Writers for

Writers for Animals

Edited by Jenny Elliott-Bennett

An anthology of animal stories written by authors from around the world, illustrated by artists from around the world, published in a collection here to raise money for two animal sanctuaries, one in England and one in Wales, and an animal rights organisation in Ireland.

Everybody who worked on this project did so as a volunteer, prompted by their desire to help animals.

All proceeds from the sale of this book will be divided evenly between the three charities.

for the animals

Bridge House

British Library Cataloguing in Publication Data

A Record of this Publication is available from the British
Library

ISBN 978-1-907335-25-9

This edition published 2012 by Bridge House Publishing
Manchester, England

All Bridge House books are published on paper derived
from sustainable resources.

These stories are intended for adults and as such the themes of some of the stories and the language are not suitable for children.

Contents

Additional animal silhouette artwork appearing
throughout by Kate Tacey

Cover designed by Chris Ledward

Introduction

Writers for Animals is a collection of stories about animals and their relationships with humans. Inspiring true-life and engaging fictional tales have been chosen, written by both published and previously unpublished authors from around the world.

The 'radical' message of this book is that animals have feelings and they have their own lives; they are not property, and their wellbeing should not be at the mercy of human whim. This book hopes to raise awareness in human society about some of the situations animals are in at our doing. This book will also raise vital funds for animal aid.

All proceeds from the sale of this book will be split evenly between three animal charities; a rescue sanctuary in England, one in Wales and an animal rights organisation in Ireland.

I have chosen these three specifically because I know the owners of the sanctuaries and the founder of the AR organisation personally, and I know that **every penny they receive goes directly to the animals**; they do not pay managers or staff – it all goes to the innocent creatures. People who buy this book can do so with complete confidence that their money will reach the abused and suffering animals that desperately need it. This book will help finance first-hand activism – literally putting food in the mouths of rescued animals and funding outreach work that changes human society for the good of non-human species.

Hillfields Animal Sanctuary, Bromsgrove, was founded over thirty years ago by Linda Tudor. It started in a small way with a few waifs and strays, ranging from pets to farm animals. The number of animals at Hillfields steadily increased and it is now home to a staggering three hundred animals, including horses, goats, pigs, sheep, chickens, dogs, fifty cats, ducks, birds and an adorable young cow, Blossom. There is also Queenie the sow, who was evicted from London Zoo because she failed to keep on reproducing; Drummer the shire horse, rescued from a meat market, who, as a foal, saw his mother slaughtered and has emotional problems as a consequence; and Truffles the piglet who was spotted lying injured under a pile of bricks at the breeder's. He was rescued and kept as a house pet for a short time until it was realised that this couldn't meet his needs. A school offered to take him, but he would've been fattened up for their fundraising hog roast. He thinks Queenie is his mum and is always up to mischief, often trying to steal the cats' food. He now spends his days rooting for apples and acorns.

Local farmers sometimes dump live male lambs in wheelie bins, because there is no money to be made from males. These poor animals lay piled up with broken limbs, left to die slowly and in agony. Lin has rescued many such lambs. She also goes to meat markets and rescues discarded creatures from bin sacks, dumped in the rubbish because they are of no financial worth to humans.

The animals at Hillfields have all been rescued from cruelty and neglect or taken in when their owners simply did not want them anymore. The sanctuary policy dictates that every animal lives out their days there, never to be moved on, free from fear of further neglect or cruelty. Linda personally tends to all the animals every day, running the sanctuary single-handedly. Her days start at five-thirty, when everybody is checked and gets breakfast, before the turning out and mucking out begins.

Hillfields have open days and fetes, animal sponsorship schemes, host fund-raising vegan meals and hold vegan bake sales and jumble sales.

Website: www.hillfields-animal-sanctuary.com

ARAN (Animal Rights Action Network) was founded more than seventeen years ago by John Carmody and is Ireland's largest animal rights group. Working internationally as well as locally, they fight to expose and stop cruelty to animals, and to promote cruelty-free living and respect for all animals.

ARAN's national and international campaigns, education programs and grassroots activism have targeted hare coursing, fur farming, Canada's baby seal slaughter, the export of Irish greyhounds to China, and Duffy's and the Courtney Brothers' animal-act circuses. ARAN has also appeared on BBC 1 television, speaking out against the UK badger slaughter. ARAN also runs an 'adopt, don't buy' advertising campaign, backed by celebrities.

John says: 'ARAN is Ireland's national animal rights group, who campaign against all forms of animal abuse, and work to promote a cruelty-free lifestyle. Thanks to ARAN's dedicated, round-the-clock voluntary work for animals in need, hearts and minds are changing faster than ever before in this country; people are now starting to question their treatment of animals. As a result of ARAN's outreach efforts, cruelty to animals issues are featured almost weekly in various press outlets all over the country, and as a result of our campaigns and education programs, more progress is being made in the fight to end animal exploitation. ARAN welcomes new members to

11

join them on their campaigns. ARAN merchandise is also available.'

Website: www.ARAN.ie

Forget-Me-Not Animal Rescue was set up in September 2010 in mid Wales. The rescue is set in three and a half acres of beautiful, untouched countryside in a very quiet area full of wildlife. The rescue centre has over fifty animals; dogs, rabbits, guinea pigs, goats and some wonderful *hennies*. The majority of these animals have all come from places where they suffered and were neglected. At Forget-Me-Not, the emphasis is on letting the animals be who they want to be. Once rescued and rehabilitated, they are given large areas to exercise in, and interesting things to do – a barren run is not what guinea pigs, rabbits or hens want or need. Watching two giant lop-eared rabbits enjoy space and sunshine for the first time was so rewarding for the rescuers, as was seeing the transformation of bedraggled and injured battery hens that turned into proud and glossy-coated, confident hennies!

Forget-Me-Not is a vegan and cruelty-free run rescue which means they do not eat animals or use anything that has been tested on them, and they encourage people to support charities that carry out animal-free progressive medical research.

Forget-Me-Not is home to a huge variety of wildlife and the founders are proud to protect wildlife habitats. They have a small lake which is home to creatures they had never even seen before, including the protected Great Crested Newt. The list of birds to be seen there is quite staggering and includes Bull Finches, Goldcrests, Red Kites, Long-tailed Tits, Wrens and Redstarts.

The centre educates people from many countries, who contact them via email asking about animal welfare. This seemingly simple outreach work is invaluable in helping improve the lives of animals around the world.

Website: www.forgetmenotanimalrescue.org.uk
Email: info@forgetmenotanimalrescue.org.uk
Tel: 07504 197588

Combating animal abuse and exploitation is an endless task because the abuse and exploitation never stops. Animals are voiceless and have no power to choose their fate for themselves; certainly no animal would offer itself to be murdered to go on our dinner tables; no animal would agree to drinking cleaning products in order to assess chemical dangers to living beings; no animal is happily skinned alive to make fur and leather accessories for us to wear; no animal dreams of being kept in a dark and filthy factory, forced to reproduce and then give up their babies for human consumption; no animal walks in from the wild and volunteers to be caged in a zoo. Animal welfare is in the hands of human beings, and too often it is ignored or deemed unimportant. The charities that this book supports are on the front line in terms of helping animals; changing human opinion about the objectification of non-human animals and animal rights, saving animal lives from abuse and neglect, offering shelter to the abandoned and stray, healing and rehabilitating the sick and injured and feeding the hungry. For the sake of the animals, buy this book and help fund the work done by these organisations.

Jenny Elliott-Bennett 2012

Dan Widdowson 2012

Cepat the Slow Loris

Elisabeth Key

You may have never heard of the slow loris.

The species' main claim to fame is that it is the world's only poisonous primate. This furry little creature with huge round eyes is as cute as they come, but its bite is toxic and can be fatal to humans. By mixing a secretion from a gland on its arm with its own saliva, the slow loris produces a poison that wards off predators and inspires myth and fear among the people of South and South East Asia, where it lives.

Sadly, the toxic bite of the slow loris isn't enough to protect it from its main predator – Man. Although its rainforest habitat is vanishing rapidly, a greater threat to the slow loris' survival is its use in traditional medicine practices. Deep-rooted beliefs about the supernatural powers of the slow loris, such as their purported ability to ward off evil spirits or cure wounds, mean huge numbers of them are caught from the wild and sold dead or alive for use in traditional medicine.

There is also an insatiable demand from the exotic pet trade to feed their popularity as pets. Their slow deliberate movements and the fact that they freeze and do nothing in dangerous situations make them a sitting target for poachers. They are sold on to illegal wildlife traders who sell them in animal markets, at the roadside and even in shopping malls. In spite of localised laws prohibiting trade in slow lorises and slow loris products, as well as protection from international commercial trade by the UN wildlife convention CITES, they are sold openly in South East Asia and smuggled to other countries, too, such as

Russia and Japan. Their popularity as pets has been boosted by viral videos on YouTube showing a captive slow loris in a Russian apartment being tickled by its giggling owner, and another gripping a small cocktail umbrella. Such clips have received millions of hits and resulted in a clamour from the public eager to know where they can buy these animals.

The method adopted by wildlife traders to turn a primate with a toxic bite into a cute and cuddly pet is chillingly simple; they remove its teeth. Ignoring the screams of pain from the terrified animal, they use a pair of nail clippers and cut them out. Such was the fate of Cepat, the Sumatran slow loris, after he was stolen from the wild.

More than half the slow lorises that have their teeth cut out die from infection or blood loss. In that respect at least, Cepat was one of the lucky ones; he survived this shocking ordeal and the trauma of the pet market in Jakarta. The cacophony of noise, the bright sunlight and his imprisonment in a small rusty cage must have been a nightmare for a shy little primate that spends its days sleeping in the cool darkness of the forest and comes to life at night to hunt for insects, birds and small mammals.

Luckily for Cepat, it wasn't long before he caught the eye of a passer-by, a local woman who couldn't resist the steady gaze of his huge brown eyes. She had never heard of a slow loris but was assured by the trader that he would make the perfect pet, requiring very little attention and able to exist on a diet of leftovers. In light of this erroneous advice, it was a miracle that Cepat survived.

But survive he did.

Now that he was a pet, the timid little slow loris was condemned to a life behind bars. His home was a barren wire cage positioned outside the front of his owner's house; she was proud of her unusual pet and wanted as many people as possible to see and admire him. Passersby were intrigued by the strange creature with the big round eyes and soft brown fur and his owner would encourage their interest and happily answer their questions about him. She would explain that her son had chosen the name Cepat for him, which means *speedy* in English (a humorous reference to his slow movements), and that he was partial to fruit but would also eat cake. Sometimes she would admit the drawback to owning a slow loris as a pet, and that was the smell, which was absolutely awful. To keep the dreadful odour at bay, Cepat was subjected to a bath every Sunday, with plenty of soap, followed by a rub down with his own special towel.

After six months of this unnatural existence, the smell of the slow loris was Cepat's salvation. His owner decided that she could bear it no longer, bath or no bath, and contacted the charity International Animal Rescue. They run a primate rehabilitation centre in Java and care for more than one hundred slow lorises rescued from the illegal pet trade.

The vet's initial assessment of Cepat was encouraging; in spite of a diet of scraps and cake, he was in good physical condition and his coat looked healthy. But sadly the sight of his tongue poking out of his mouth confirmed what his rescuers had feared – Cepat's teeth had been cut out, making it impossible for him ever to fend for himself in the wild.

In spite of this sad news, the future is looking bright for Cepat. At least in the rescue centre he can behave as he would in the wild, passing slowly and silently through the cool, dark foliage that has been provided to recreate his natural habitat in the forest. He can sleep all day and hunt for food all night, pouncing on insects and small animals with astonishing speed and dexterity. He will no longer be gawped at or held and squeezed by inexpert hands. And he will no longer have to endure being bathed once a week.

How ironic that this extraordinary primate with the poisonous bite to protect it from predators should ultimately be saved from a lifetime in a small cage by nothing worse than a nasty smell!

Mortimer Sparrow 2012

Amazing Gracie!

Sarah Brown

I first set eyes on Gracie when we went to rescue some ex-battery hens. We had set up our own small animal rescue a few months previously and were now ready to start taking on animals. I had promised myself a long time ago, when the idea of running my own rescue was formulating in my head, that hens farmed in the horrendous factory system would be the first we rescued, and they were!

We arrived at the farm and watched them off-load hundreds of hens in crates. A tiny bald hen caught my eye. She was desperately trying to make herself invisible in the corner of her crate. I instantly wanted to take her home with us, along with all the other hens in the same crate; sixteen tiny little lives altogether.

We emptied the crate of hens, one by one, gently putting them in the hutches we had brought to transport them in. As Gracie was handed to me I noticed that she held her head at a strange angle, and looking at her right eye I saw that she was blind; only one good eye and the tiniest body ever – my maternal instincts took over and she was to become my friend for life.

Arriving back at our rescue, we carried the hutches into the shed where we had prepared a large pen for the hens' arrival. We left the hutch doors open so that they could come out and explore in their own time, rather than having the trauma of being handled again. With hutches at both ends of the shed, we held our breath and waited… and waited… but not one little hen ventured out; it was all too much.

Patiently we waited for over half an hour for the first brave hen to step foot into their forever home, and to our utter amazement Gracie was to be the bravest hen of all! She stepped out on to the deep bed of wood shavings and gazed about, holding her head at the crooked angle that we would become so familiar with over the next few months. She took a few steps forward and started eating. It was probably the first meal she'd had in a long time without having to fear the bullying from her cage-mates, as they were all still in the hutch!

Despite her initial bravery, Gracie was pretty much scared of everyone. I dread to think what it was like for her and all the other hens imprisoned in the cages they are forced to exist in for their entire lives. It really is barbaric. Sadly, our second group of rescued battery hens really were a poorly lot; many couldn't stand and were so weak we had to hand feed them for a good while. Again we rescued sixteen, but this time we weren't so fortunate and we lost one of our little ones. We had called her Speedy as she zoomed about everywhere despite a leg that was obviously not quite right. She had seventeen days of freedom with us and she died in our garden, with the sun warming her face; a tragedy for her and for us.

After this heartbreak we thought that we should try to put Gracie in with our second group of rescued hennies, along with another hen, Fluffy Chest, who we had paired her up with away from the others who picked on them. It was the best decision ever! Compared to the new hens, Gracie and Fluffy Chest were large and well-feathered and straight away they were seen as boss hennies. It actually made me cry to see Gracie strutting her stuff amongst a group of hens as we had only ever seen her duck (or should I say 'hen and dive'?) away from hens before, as they all picked on her. She is still boss lady and the other hens respect her, just like we do.

22

Every day we call her name and she comes running across the grass to see us. She really does respond to her name, and will raise her head and speak to us when we walk past and follow us to the shed where she knows the food bins are! When we first saw her in a roost making a nest to lay her first egg, it was incredible. Her voice after the event was loud and proud as if she was saying 'Look what I've just done!' It was a very special moment for us, exactly six months after taking this wonderful hen home with us. She loves a gentle cuddle before she goes to bed at night, showing complete trust by closing her eyes and relaxing in my arms after a hard day foraging in the field!

I wish that there wasn't a need to rescue any animal, and that they all lived free and happy lives without human interference... but until that day arrives we will continue to live a vegan life and do all we can to help people become aware of how amazing and truly individual ALL Gracies – who are so brutally treated in their billions by the farming system – are in every way.

Lucy Thornton 2012

Blackbird

Catherine Ione Gray

As a young girl, I spent many hours during the summer breaks from school watching wildlife. I grew up in a semi-rural town in Michigan in the United States, where we used to have many regular visitors to the garden; birds, raccoons, opossums, black and red squirrels, and very occasionally white tailed deer. Michigan is a fabulous place to see wildlife, both flora and fauna, due to its abundance of forest and freshwater ecosystems. But it is not the best place for the wildlife, as it also has a high proportion of hunters.

I moved to England in later life. I soon found myself again feeding the birds and other wildlife that entered our garden. Even in our semi-detached property just outside of a busy town, we had many visitors to our garden. In such a built-up area I knew we were lucky to be able to take countless photos of foxes, hedgehogs and many different types of birds.

Two years ago, we were able to move into the country. It didn't take me long to start up my feeding ritual. One feeder became two, and so on, and now I have six feeding stations dotted around the garden. Such wildlife we get, that I have to refill them at least twice a day. We have a wide range of birds that visit, from the prevalent sparrow, blackbird and wood pigeon to the slightly more unusual long tailed tit, golden finch and yellow hammer. We also have a pond which newts and frogs live in happily, a fox that wanders in, a hedgehog that snuffles about, a brown rat that has over-wintered in our compost bin and so many pheasants I could not possibly even guess at a number.

I tend to think of the animals as a part of my family and feel a responsibility towards them that is quite maternal. There are days when I walk around the garden to find the perished body of one of my brood. As an adult I understand the world as it is and realise all animals die at some point, but my heart sinks with each animal that perishes; even though I had never known him or her, my heart still weeps at the loss of innocent life.

In June of last year, I returned home from work and went to fill the bird feeders as per my usual routine. I was actually early home from work for once and though it was a few hours earlier than usual, thought I'd make my rounds at any rate. I started in the front garden, filling each station with mixed seed, nuts and dried fruit as needed and moved on. As I rounded the corner towards the back of the garden, I stopped; inside one of my bird feeders was a bird, and he wasn't moving.

The bird feeder was actually a feeder for nuts, so it was a metal tube about four to five centimetres in diameter, and about twenty-five centimetres long. The lid had broken off it and although I had kept replacing it, it had obviously come off again in the wind. There was only a small smattering of food at the bottom of the tube and the blackbird had obviously decided he would try his luck and had climbed into the feeder, head first.

I approached the feeder with a heavy heart, and cursed myself for being party to his death. How foolish I had been not to have secured the lid properly. But as I approached the feeder, the bird's eyes focused on me. He was alive. I can't tell you what relief and joy I felt at

26

seeing him look at me, but I knew that he was suffering, so I quickly ran into the house.

At first I panicked. How do I get him out of the bird feeder without hurting him? I also knew I had no idea how long he had been in the feeder. He could have been in since the early morning (the last time I had looked out at the garden), and being in the balmy June weather all that time, he could be dehydrated and on the verge of death.

Quickly I grabbed the first thing I came upon and rushed back outside. I unhooked the tube and laid him on the grass so that he at least was no longer suspended upside-down. He watched me. I talked calmly to him as I took the scissors and prayed they were strong enough to cut the wire mesh prison. Slowly I cut one rung, then two, then three. As I did so, I turned the edges over, winding them down the bird. It took me ages to cut, each cut having to be made with force, but precisely and gently for fear of harming the bird inside. Finally I had cut a little more than half-way down the feeder. As I turned the edges back, the bird's legs were freed and he was able to wiggle the rest of his body out. He hopped about on the ground and then flew off into the brush, finally free from his prison.

For the next few days I watched for the bird again. It was sometime later and we were in the vegetable patch of the garden when a blackbird came. By the way he looked at me, I believed it was the same one. I quickly retrieved dried fruit from inside the house and returned to find him waiting for me.

For many weeks after the incident, every time I went outside the blackbird appeared. I always dropped some dried fruit on the ground, but he never seemed very interested in the fruit. Perhaps he was trying to thank me for what I had done; who can say for certain? I like to think he's out there in our garden, teaching his children that some humans are friendly and that they should never, ever climb into a tight place head first... even if the nuts at the bottom do look tasty.

Dan Widdowson 2012

Felinology

Jenny Elliott-Bennett

I adopted Tigger from the local animal shelter. He was a bit bigger than the other kittens there, and I assumed this indicated that he was a bit older than them. I called him Tigger because of his tabby coat; striped like a tiger.

I bought several types of food for him to try, fearing he might be a fussy eater. He ate all of them in a single sitting. He even had enough appetite left to help me with my own dinner.

I thought that because he was big he'd soon stop growing, but I was wrong. He had a tremendous appetite and swelled enormously; he was soon bigger than any of the other cats in the neighbourhood.

One morning there was a knock on my door; I was amazed to see it was a policeman.

'Can I help you?'

'It's about your tiger, Miss,' he said.

'He's called Tigger, not Tiger,' I corrected.

'I shall make note of his name, Miss, but my main concern is the fact that you have a fully grown tiger and that he's been bothering the neighbourhood.'

'He's not a tiger, he's a tabby.'

'May I see,' he paused to consult his notebook, 'this *Tigger?*'

I took the policeman through to Tigger's room, where he was curled up, sleeping.

'You see, Miss, if he was a common domestic cat, your Tigger would be approximately a foot and a half long from nose to tail-tip. The fact that he is ten feet long and has teeth like carving knives suggests that he is, in fact, a fully grown tiger.'

'Fully grown, is he? I was wondering how big he would get.'

'You're missing my point. We've had a series of complaints – he is roaming freely around and scaring the public.'

'Oh.'

'If he were any other animal than a tiger, I would issue an order for his destruction because he is a nuisance and a threat to the local populace. However, as tigers are a protected species—' I hurriedly interjected at that point, 'Oh yes, in which case he is *definitely* a tiger.'

'Thank you, Miss, I needed that corroboration. As I was saying, tigers are a protected species, so I can only request that you to take greater care over his whereabouts.'

He handed me a piece of paper. 'What's this?'

'It's a tiger ASBO. It means that if he's ever out of the house again, he'll be taken away and put in a zoo.'

'But little Tigger loves to go out and stretch his legs at all times of the day and night! He loves to play with the neighbourhood cats! I couldn't possibly keep him locked in.'

I eventually managed to shoo the policeman away, with an assurance that Tigger would remain within the house and garden. I hoped I would never see him again. I certainly little expected to have to telephone the policeman the next day.

'Ah, it's you, Miss. Problems with your tiger? Would you like me to arrange for a zoo to help you out?'

'Not at all; Tigger's been as good as gold. In fact, he's

been the perfect guard cat and caught a couple of burglars.'

'Burglars?'

'Yes, I woke up and went downstairs to find two ruffi-
ans with a bagful of my stuff, lying flat-out on the floor
with Tigger on top of them.'

'They're still there, then?'

'Oh, yes. Tigger's looking after them. Would you
come and collect them?'

On the following day I answered the door to find the same
policeman standing there again. This time he was holding
a big, gold medallion on a purple sash.

'Congratulations, Miss,' he said, 'I bring good news.
Your tiger is a hero; he stopped a bank raid.'

'A bank raid?'

'Yes. We have the CCTV footage to prove it. Three
members of a notorious local gang forced their way into
the safe of the bank on the High Street. A tiger in a
President Obama mask went in, disarmed them and lay on
top of them until we arrived. It was in very much the same
way as he caught your burglars yesterday.'

'Officer, if he was wearing an Obama mask you don't
know that it was *my* Tigger. It could have been *any* tiger,
or large tabby cat.'

'I checked the local census, Miss. Tigger is the only
tiger in the district. He's a hero now, look, and the Mayor
asked me to present him with this medal.'

I wasn't convinced. 'Well, if it wasn't another tiger,
maybe it was President Obama dressed in a tiger suit.
Have you thought of that?'

He insisted on coming in to present the medal. 'Ah,
look at this,' he cried, 'a President Obama mask in
Tigger's basket.'

'That doesn't prove anything,' I said. 'I saw a child wearing a mask like that just yesterday.'

'Yes, a child, but not a tiger.'

Well thank goodness that's over, I thought, when he finally left. I could do with not seeing that officer again for another ten years. But, sure enough, he was back again the next day, clutching yet another medallion. 'Obamatiger struck again, Miss,' he said.

'Obamatiger?'

'It's what the newspapers are calling him. This time he saved the entire town from destruction. You see, a billionaire oil tycoon was out on a jolly in his helicopter, but lost control of the thing. The chopper was plummeting towards the gas works. If it had hit, the explosion would have reduced five square miles to rubble. A tiger, wearing an Obama mask, flew up to the helicopter, wrestled with the controls, and saved us all.'

'But Tigger can't fly. He can *bounce*, but he can't fly.'

'I can quote witness statements, Miss. "There was some initial confusion as to the identity of our saviour. It was suggested that it might be a bird, or even a plane, before it was realised that it was in fact a tiger in a President Obama mask that had flown to our rescue." '

The policeman left another medal, even though I protested again that my little Tigger couldn't fly. Everyone makes such a fuss and says that my little Tigger is really Obamatiger, but I think that's nonsense. Just look at him, curled up in his basket. Does he really look like a superhero to you? He's just my little tabby cat.

Mortimer Sparrow 2012

Gods of the Rivers and the Sky

Stephen Wade

Hidden behind a snarl of brambles, perched among the newly-sprouted leaves on a young whitethorn tree, Conawk the merlin, a small falcon the size of a blackbird, watched, fascinated, a kingfisher doing what kingfishers do. The kingfisher, a blue and orange bird, was happily fishing on the far side of the riverbank.

Conawk had heard of these birds from his parents. His parents had never in their lives seen one of these curious-looking birds, but had described them to him in bedtime stories back in the days before Conawk fledged. They, too, had heard about the kingfisher from their parents, long before their wings had stiffened and their talons had grown strong. Kingfisher meat was unpleasant to eat, they'd told him. But for now curiosity overrode Conawk's hunger concerns.

Never had Conawk imagined there could be a creature whose dazzling feathers were as brilliant as the sun and bluer than the turquoise-blue in a rainbow.

Bobbing its head once then twice and flicking its small tail, the colourful kingfisher left its perch and dived into the still waters of a deep inlet. To the sounds of the summer's evening – the trilling birdsong, the humming wind, bleating sheep and the occasional, distant, braying donkey, all accompanied by the whispering waters – the small bird's body breaking the river's surface added a satisfying plop-note; a note that was repeated, though in reverse, with added plink-plonks made by water-droplets, as the bird left the river and returned to its perch, a silver fish wriggling in its long, thin bill.

Conawk's rumbling stomach reminded him of his true

purpose – the need to feed so that he could make it through the night. The night, a time when the fire in the sky disappeared and left his body trembling, the way he had trembled that time Tertius the peregrine – the Prince of Falcons – with his deadly yellow talons curled and ready, almost tore Conawk from the sky. Conawk shuddered.

Ruffling away the memory, Conawk then slipped off his own perch and powered, low and fast, across the river, cutting the air like white light. The blue and orange bird screeched and tried to dive to safety.

Too late.

At eight seasons, about twenty in bird years, Conawk was a practised hunter and, without thinking, shifted his flight pattern, dipped under his target's perch and grasped the escaping bird with his outstretched talons.

From a confusion of reeds, leaves and loose feathers, Conawk righted himself and dragged his prey up the river bank to level ground, where he could pluck it before settling down to eat his meal. The force of Conawk's speedy strike had left the kingfisher dazed or unconscious. Perfect.

On the riverbank, out of sight behind a rotting log and long grass, Conawk tilted his head, this way and that. His telescopic vision boring through the thick vegetation and scouring the skies for danger, and, at the same time, he keenly listened beyond the scolding wind and the tinkling, indifferent river. The river that would keep on running its course, ignoring even the drowning cries of a bird with waterlogged feathers.

'Ooooooh,' the wind said to Conawk, raising its voice. 'Bad bird! Taker of life. River rustler. Destroyer of the innocent.' It then raised its voice higher, making the trees shudder, and blew into Conawk's face so hard he had to fasten onto the grass with his free foot, the one that wasn't pinning his prey, and squeeze his eyes shut until the wind spent its angry mood, settled down and snaked off over the river, into the trees.

A new sound, but a sound with which Conawk was well acquainted, rose up from the earth. Tiny voices, focused and fearless, encouraged each other that food had fallen their way, enough food to feed ten thousand. Conawk could smell them, too. Their scent was as sharp and strong as their self-belief, and their determination was awesome: an army of ants.

'Come on,' the ant leader commanded. 'No slacking. Anybody who can't keep up will be left behind.' On they marched, the ant army.

Conawk opened his pointed wings, flapped, jumped and scrambled onto the moss-covered log, pulling with him the blue and orange kingfisher. Atop the log, this new position gave him plenty of time to feast uninterrupted.

Unrelenting, the ant-Sergeant halted his squadron, and, before resuming an advancing attack up the log from three separate angles, he split his regiment into three bands. As a lone hunter, Conawk couldn't understand the tiny creatures' loyalty to each other, but he admired their persistence.

He was settling down to pluck feathers when the bird under Conawk's talons stirred. Instinctively he clenched his prey tighter, causing the little bird's black eyes to pop open.

'*Chickee,*' she screamed, which meant '*Help*' in a language understood only by wild birds and animals.

A strange, stabbing pain shot through Conawk's chest. It was a feeling he might have felt if Tertius the Prince of Falcon's great talons had punctured his breast and pierced his heart.

'*Chee chee,*' the kingfisher cried. 'Don't hurt me, Sir. Please, don't hurt me.'

Not knowing why, Conawk released the kingfisher and hopped aside. Perhaps it was because she had confused him by calling him *Sir* – *Sir* was how Conawk had addressed his own father in the early months. Or perhaps he had remembered, without remembering, that kingfisher flesh didn't taste good.

Conawk's hunger was now replaced by a thirst that went beyond the need for liquid. 'Who are you?' he said. 'And why do you call me 'Sir'? I am not my father.'

The little bird's body shivered as though it were deep winter and not a day warm enough to awaken swarms of humming bumblebees, a day that roused and transformed the caterpillars from their winter sleep into flitting butterflies. 'My wing,' the kingfisher said. 'I can't move my wing. I think it's broken.'

He looked at the little bird's wing hanging helplessly by her side, blood seeping into her feathers from a wound on her shoulder, knowing that he was the cause of her injury. Conawk apologised, 'Forgive me,' he said. This was the first time he had apologised to anyone in his two long years of life. The kingfisher, he knew, needed her wings in order to fly and dive for fish. Without the use of her wings, she would die. 'The wind must be cruel on your open wound,' he added. He then stepped closer and tried to mantle her with his wings.

'Mama,' her high-pitched whistle called. 'Chickee. Mama. Papa.'

'Hush,' Conawk said. 'You'll draw the others here.'

But the others were already gathering. The first to arrive was a charm of goldfinches. The finches chirped and twittered their disapproval at Conawk, first for being a falcon, and then for his murderous attack on the kingfisher. Backed up by a parcel of linnets and a bellowing of bullfinches that flew in from the nearby thistle patch, the goldfinches bounced and darted about more like a swarm of flies than a flock of birds. The small birds screeched at Conawk as they swooped for his ducking head, aiming to graze him with their pointy beaks. 'Tswitt-witt-witt,' they shrieked in unison. 'Go back to where you belong.'

Torn between the instinct to flee from the mob and the strange urge compelling him to stay and make amends for the damage he'd caused to the kingfisher, this beautiful creature that wasn't his natural prey, Conawk's decision was made for him when the heavyweights arrived; a raucous murder of hooded crows, and a cackling tribe of magpies. They jeered and taunted him, not that these uniformed bandits really cared whether he harmed the kingfisher or not.

Conawk could see that the black and white and shady presence of these living demons was causing the kingfisher even greater terror. She had collapsed onto her breast, and lay there, open-beaked, one wing outstretched before her, the other unnaturally limp by her side. Normally she would have fled to safety as the first silver-lined silhouette came between her and the sun.

'Ki-ki-ki-ki-ki-ki,' Conawk screamed unexpectedly, and in a tone so high-pitched and commanding, every bird, from the tiniest goldcrest to the raggedy heron, fell silent; the howling wind lost its voice, and even the whispering, indifferent river stopped its babbling. The river animals, too, left off their rummaging, swimming, paddling and burrowing in their endless quest to feed themselves and their young.

Out of the water shot the sleek-brown mother otter. She held her quizzical head aloft, drinking in all the commotion. Behind her bounded her five cubs. They had abandoned their water acrobatics, only to continue, on land, their ceaseless games of wrestling, chasing and being chased. Unlike their mother, the otter cubs showed neither interest in nor respect for what Conawk had to say.

Drawn too by Conawk's piercing cry came the stoat, who had been on the trail of a field mouse farther down the riverbank. The stoat moved through the long, undulating grass. With great caution when he neared the unusual gathering of animals and birds encircling the log, the stoat slinked his way through feather, fur and feet to the front of the inner circle. There the better to take in the words, words that cracked like sparks in a forest fire, crackling from Conawk's beak.

Sensing the stoat was no longer about, the fieldmouse slipped out of its hiding place; a burrow in the riverbank that contained at its end a collection of fish-bones, too tightly packed for a stoat to penetrate.

Few of the animals or birds present noticed the dainty fieldmouse who, retaining survival instinct enough to avoid clumsy feet and potentially dangerous beaks, stopped outside the circle and cautiously made his way up a tall reed growing at the river's edge. From there he jumped into the unkempt hair of a willow tree. The willow tree shook her leafy locks from her face, squinted her wrinkled eyes at her uninvited guest, and then returned to her gentle weeping.

'Back away, birds and beasts,' Conawk said. 'Ki-ki-ki-ki-ki.' He jerked about on one spot in a kind of manic dance, wings flapping, covering all points of the compass, to face-down his tormentors. 'Bigger than me some of you are,' Conawk continued. 'Stronger in shoulder, and sharper in tooth, bill and claw I cannot deny. But afraid of you, whether you are a noble killer who hunts alone or a coward who attacks from behind the protection of a thousand, I am not.'

42

'Who is this puny braggart?' cawed a young crow that had only recently sprouted adult plumage.

'Be careful!' an older crow warned the younger one. 'Never ever discount the claims screeched by a falcon under threat.'

But the younger crow, who had images of himself as a fearless raven, and fancied he was some kind of avenging black angel, unfurled his wings and flung himself at Conawk. 'Release her, son of an albino blackbird,' the crow said. 'You robin and swallow hybrid.'

But Conawk, who had already released the kingfisher, side-stepped the attacking crow, back-snapped a long yellow leg and caught the crow's head in his talons. An agonised, deep-base caw ripped from the crow's throat as he fell from the log with Conawk's talons and Conawk attached to his head and neck. He thrashed about in the decimated circle of fleeing creatures.

'Don't move, son,' the old crow shouted to the younger. Advice to which the younger paid no heed.

'Listen to the old man,' Conawk screeched. 'Ki-ki-ki-ki. Stay down or you'll lose the other one.'

Amidst their wrestling bodies and flapping wings, Conawk was aware of the circling animals and birds once more advancing inward. 'Back off!' he warned. 'Any closer and Gunner here loses the other eye.'

A murmuring snaked through the crowd. The finches, like animated fruit dotting the surrounding trees in hundreds, twittered their agreement to stock up on oil-rich seeds before bedtime. For them, the show was over. The low-hanging sun watched the retreating finch-flocks, and from the flying clusters cast elongated, sailing shadows across the earth.

43

In the background, the frog and toad parties had begun their evening croaking: rehearsals for the night-time. The very scent of imminent darkness swirled about in the wind. The wind had found his voice again and was now wailing away the remains of the day. Likewise the river was once more wending its way, babbling fiercely, on its endless course.

The mother otter had seen enough. Aping the beckoning river, she called her brood. Soon the last audience member left was the old crow. Finally he, too, departed. His favourite perching spot in the rookery was by now probably taken. And he was getting far too old for bickering and battling with his fellows. His last advice to the young crow was to take to the undergrowth as soon as Conawk detached his talons from the young bird's empty eye-socket. Rest, he advised the young crow, was the one flight-route remaining for survival. 'Lie low,' he said. 'Keep near the running water. You'll need to drink. Drink and sleep. And sleep long.'

'Kaa-kaa-kaa-kaa,' the young crow cawed. 'I'm blind. My colours are gone. There are no more shapes. He's taken my eyes.'

'No,' the old crow shouted back at him. 'Hear me on this, son. You still have one good eye. Do as I tell you and you'll keep that eye. One eye is more eyes than have all the bats and all the moles together in every land.'

Conawk reminded the young crow that the departing advice of his adoptive mentor was all that remained to keep him in the natural world that moved between light and dark, and to save him from one of perpetual darkness.

'Okay,' the young crow said to Conawk. 'Ka-ka-ka. You win. Okay. You win.'

Carefully detaching his talons from the other bird's head and neck, Conawk hopped back onto the log next to where the kingfisher, exhausted, it seemed, still lay. Before turning his attentions to her, he watched the young crow thrashing off into the undergrowth. 'Ki-ki-ki-ki-ki,' Conawk screeched after him – a subtle reminder.

With just he and the kingfisher alone on the log by the riverbank, Conawk could finally tend to her. But something was wrong. When he tilted his head in her direction, there was panic in her dark eyes. From the bony light thrown by the waking moon, he could make them out: tiny red bodies, intent on staking their claim, were clambering about her feathers. Some had made it to her open shoulder wound. She was under attack – the ant army.

Futile to attempt to reason with ants – ants never listen. Conawk pecked lightly at the foot soldiers in the kingfisher's feathers, breaking their backs, and spat them aside. He scratched with his deadly talons the advancing troops from the log, until he heard the tiny voice of the ant sergeant commanding his squad to fall back and retreat.

He spat out the bitter, pungent taste from his mouth. Conawk mantled the kingfisher's shivering body by stretching his wings over and around her to protect her from the cold of night-time. This time she did not protest. All night he lay awake like this, ready to defend her from the creatures that preferred the moon to the sun. But even the moon creatures stayed away.

Dawn arrived, and the sun. The humming wings of dragonflies hawking insects over the sleepless river replaced the croaking toads. And the hoots and screeches made by owls gave way to trilling birdsong, proclaiming and reclaiming territory. Conawk stepped aside and allowed the sun's wayward kisses to stir the kingfisher from her sleep.

'You,' she said. 'You stayed with me. I don't understand.'

Conawk didn't understand either. It seemed the thing to do, the way eating was what you did when hungry and resting when tired. 'You never told me your name,' he said.

'Florissa,' she said. And she smiled a smile that only other birds could see.

That smile faded quickly. A silver fish jumping clear of the water next to the log brought with it the reality of her injuries and her inability to fish.

'I'll be back,' Conawk said impulsively, slicing through the air to hunt down breakfast. How difficult could catching a few measly fish be? A seasoned hunter, who was swift enough to take small birds on the wing; he who could spot his prey from a great distance, rocket after and seize a fleeing shrew or a mouse from the ground before it reached its burrow. But catching fish, he discovered, proved far more difficult than he could have imagined.

The fish he dived after disappeared before his feet even grazed the water. And then his feathers were waterlogged, and it was necessary to find an open perch and dry his wings like a cormorant or a heron. A heron! That was it. When his feathers had dried-out, he left his perch and zipped downriver to where the heron was fishing in the shallows. At first he asked her nicely for a few minnows.

'Get lost, maggot,' the heron said. 'I have enough to contend with what with those black demons from the rookery hassling me every evening when I'm flying home.'

He asked the heron if she'd heard about the young crow that was half-blinded by a falcon before the rising of the last moon. She had. But so what?

The heron stretched out her neck and listened more intently while Conawk explained that he was the falcon responsible for the young crow's condition. He put an offer to her: in exchange for a few small fish every day, he promised to accompany her and to keep the crows at bay during her journey home to the high trees down river.

'Kraaarnk,' the heron said, because she was a bird who didn't like to waste time. 'Done.' She straightaway speared a small roach and tossed it to Conawk.

'This is for you, Florissa,' Conawk said, on his return to the log. Too weak yet to swallow the fish whole, Conawk tore it into small strips for Florissa, which he then placed into her open beak. If birds were capable of it, Conawk's cheeks would have burned bright red; a red redder than the red that sometimes bled from the evening sky.

Many moons came and were chased away by the lilac-robed dawn and the fiery sun before Florissa was once more able to fish for her own breakfast. By then a strong bond had developed between Conawk and Florissa. They were inseparable.

More an understanding than a rule, Conawk and Florissa knew that there would be consequences even before they began, in secret, to gather nesting material to shape into a summer home where they could raise a family. Their choice of home brought the first tension that threatened the relationship between the strange couple.

Conawk's preference was to move off to the cliffs by the sea and set up a home on a rocky ledge. Florissa's dream was to dig a tunnel into the riverbank and furnish the inner chamber with fish bones. They compromised, and created their unorthodox home in the hollowed-out log where they'd first met.

As expected, they were criticised by the others. Along with the almost constant twittered abuse from the garish flocks of finches, they endured screeched and shrieked insults from the otter and the blackbird. Ducks quacked at them, geese honked, and even the saintly-looking swans hissed their disapproval, stretching their s-shaped necks skyward as the falcon and kingfisher flew by.

Conawk and Florissa sensed that things would be far worse when their young were hatched. But Conawk reassured Florissa; had not he fended off the murderous crows, kept the curious otter, the bloodthirsty stoat and an army of ravenous ants at bay? Even Prince Tertius the peregrine had commended Conawk since hearing about his standoff with the beasts and birds. And, although Tertius didn't understand the attraction Conawk felt for Florissa, he gave him his approval; should ever Conawk need a strong right wing, Tertius had promised him... 'kek-kek-kek-kek-kek'... he could depend on him.

'Worry not,' Conawk whispered in Florissa's ear as she settled down to brood their six white-brown eggs. 'Our chicks will be unique; multi-talented fishermen and hunters. And with your beauty and my... ki-ki-ki-ki...' he cleared his throat... 'speed, others will in time come to respect them for what they are; true masters of the air and water; birds for whom the skies and rivers were formed.'

Dan Widdowson 2012

Gulliver Travels

Patricia Stoner

July. The south of France. It was hot. Nothing stirred.

The village children had stopped yelling. The good ol' boys had left their bench under the plane tree in the square and gone home for their midday *pain et vin*. Lizards were curled up in the cracks in our dry stone wall, dreaming no doubt of juicy grapes.

We had finished our lunch and the water in our glasses was growing tepid; the bubbles flat and the ice a distant memory. The afternoon stretched before us. Thoughts of siestas in cool shuttered rooms were beginning to coax us from our lethargy.

Then, in quick succession, there was a *whirr*, a shout of alarm from Himself, a scrabble, a squeak, a slither and a thump. A small, angry bundle of fluff and feathers sat on the table and glared at us. Gulliver had arrived.

Of course, we didn't know at the time that it was Gulliver. We didn't in fact know *what* he was, although we realised his parents probably belonged to the summer-visitor group. Our terrace was loomed over by the crumbling tower of the village's thirteenth century church. Every summer hundreds of birds would gather and nest there, and every evening they would emerge for the feeding frenzy.

Imagine if you will a gang of small boys of five or six or seven, congregating on the corner proudly with new Christmas bicycles. They gather, they chatter, then suddenly *whee!* They're off, pedalling furiously, shrieking, laughing, swooping down the street and around the corner… such were our summer visitors.

We often debated their species: swifts, swallows, house

51

martins? What use bird books and details of markings when all we saw of them were fast-moving silhouettes against a dazzling or darkening sky?

Then we found the answer. Swifts, according to the bird book, have *'vigorous, dashing flight, wheeling, winnowing and gliding; excited parties chase each other squealing around the houses in small towns and villages'*. Yes! That was just how our summer birds behaved.

The birds would cease flight only to nest and lay their eggs. Year after year we would see their offspring make their first tentative forays into the wider world, to the anxious encouragement of their parents. During our summers in France we had seen many baby casualties who had launched themselves from high roosts on unsteady wings and optimism. Sadly many came to grief, and not all survived the adventure.

Now here was Gulliver.

We quickly named him so, because of his heroic travels and because, well, if he was a swift, the name was perfectly appropriate. Mind you, he didn't look remotely like what the bird book said a swift should look like: *'an all-black bird with graceful swept-back wings and a forked tail'*. His tail was stubby and he had a fawn band on his back and a fawn underbelly. But he was a baby, so perhaps he would grow into the bird-book image.

The immediate problem was what to do with him. I found a small cardboard box and crumpled some paper towel into it, then scooped him up and put him in. He didn't seem too grateful for the rescue. In fact, he tried to peck me.

We settled him in the shade on the wide window sill

and left him to recover from the shock of his crash. At seven o'clock, the time the locals called *l'heurebleue*, when the birds and then the bats emerged from their siestas, I went to look at him. Astonishingly, he was still alive. I let him out of the box, hoping that he would find his wings, but he did no such thing. He just squatted on the window sill, glaring at me. I had no idea what to feed a baby bird, so I tried him with a crumb of sandwich, with a bit of lettuce still clinging to it. It disappeared in no time, so I fed him some more. Now there was the question of water. Do birds drink? I put a saucer of water beside him. He surveyed it balefully for a moment, and then turned his back. I turned him around and dunked his beak in the water, careful not to fill his nostrils.

We had Gulliver for over a week. We kept him in his cardboard box in the shade on the wide window sill all day, and in the evenings encouraged him to explore and try out his wings. We taught him to drink water. We continued to feed him on table scraps. The one time I managed to catch an insect he turned up his beak at it.

At first he showed no interest in flying. When his aunts and brothers and cousins swooped overhead in their ceaseless quest for insects, he would look up at them scornfully, as if to say, 'You have to *work* for a living?'

Then one day he went missing.

I hunted frantically and finally found him at the foot of the cellar stairs. He must have flown down, because as far as I could see he was uninjured. Flying back, however, seemed to be beyond him. 'Well, what are you going to do about it?' was the clear challenge in his stare. I returned him to the patio. It was a turning point, though. No more heroic dives down the cellar steps, but every evening he would creep to the edge of the window sill and try out his wings, inevitably crash-landing in a heap of indignant feathers. Every evening he flew a little further.

One afternoon I was on the terrace, sunbathing. Suddenly Gulliver began to climb up the house wall. Sensing something was afoot, I called urgently to my husband, 'You'd better get out here fast. I think Baby is leaving home.' Gulliver climbed on up steadily until he reached the guttering on the roof. Then he turned and looked at us. I could almost hear him say, 'Watch me! Mum! Dad! Watch me!' He launched himself into space. We held our breath. He tumbled through the air and we tensed for a rescue mission. He began to climb, airborne this time. As he rounded the church another bird swooped down and flew beside him. We felt proud and tearful – we had reared our first chick.

Edd Cross 2012

King Kong

Teresa Ashby

I'd know those clattering heels anywhere and as I straighten up with my bucket of disinfectant, I see Gina tottering towards me with a furry pink handbag dangling from her finger.

I shouldn't be surprised to see her. After all, she's only had two holidays so far this year and goodness me, it's almost the summer already. Oh, mustn't forget the short break she had at a health spa to recharge her poor, worn out batteries and the romantic weekend in Paris with her husband (or it may have been with someone else's, you never know with Gina).

'Maria,' she sniffs, not even bothering to add a greeting or even a smile. 'Amazed to see you're still here. Haven't you been able to find a proper job yet?'

I don't bother telling her that this is a proper job. The best job in the world as far as I'm concerned.

'Kong will be pleased to see you, anyway,' she says, rather icily, as if to let me know that she isn't. Kong is a beautiful Shar-Pei. I have no doubt that Gina bought him as a fashion accessory.

'How long are you off for this time?' I ask.

'Just a week,' she says gaily. 'Toodle-oo. Have fun with your mucking out.' And off she goes.

Resisting the temptation to whack her across the behind with my stiff-bristle brush is harder than you can imagine. Most people who drop their dogs off here leave if not in tears, then looking rather sad. But not Gina. I've known people sneak back just to check that their dog or cat has settled down. And there are those that come back from holiday early or phone every day while they're away.

And it isn't unheard of for someone to rush back in floods of tears saying they've cancelled their holiday because they just can't bear to leave their Beloved behind! Meanwhile, Beloved is probably having the time of his life chatting up the glamorous Bichon Frise in the next pen.

I hurry round to see Kong. He is a magnificent dog, powerfully built and handsome. Well, I think so, even though Gina calls him an ugly old wrinkly slobber chops. He's neither old nor ugly, and I don't mind the slobbering. It doesn't bother Gina that she thinks he's ugly because he cost a lot of money and no-one she knows has got one anything like him. Status symbol, you see. Kong is a head turner.

He's sitting leaning up against the wire door of his pen, his loose skin all bunched up as he looks in the opposite direction. He's not gazing longingly after Gina, but rather hungrily towards the food store.

'Kong,' I say and he leaps up and whirls round in a frenzy of joy. I think he might be as happy to see me as I am him. Well I don't know why I've fallen for him, do I? But Kong is here rather more often than most of our guests and I've gotten to know him rather well.

I enter his pen and make a fuss of him, running my hands over his thick harsh coat. Shar-Pei's are definitely people dogs. They love the company of humans and Kong is no exception. He's calm, but affectionate and not at all aloof which is what makes staying here so difficult for him.

I've finished cleaning out, so I decide to take Kong for a good walk. Gina thinks taking a dog for a walk means sticking him in the back of her car, driving him to a field and letting him run round for five minutes while she poses prettily for her admirers.

I take him with Snuffles, a dear little Pekinese who comes in every year while her mum goes off to visit her sister in Spain for a fortnight and Mr Churchill, a bulldog of course, who is here while his dad is in hospital having a knee replaced.

Some dogs positively love coming here. They love the company of other dogs and the rewards they get from their guilt-ridden families when they are collected. Some, like Kong, just seem to accept it as their lot in life. For Kong, this is his home from home.

At the end of the week, Gina swans back – a day late which isn't unusual. She wafts into the office so she can tell Dora all about her 'Marvellous holiday, darling,' and 'Madeira was simply divine, as always.'

I'm outside and I can hear every word. She hasn't even asked if Kong is all right. In fact, it's so long since she's drawn breath it's a wonder she's not flat-out on the floor, getting dust and dog fur stuck to her well-oiled suntan.

Kong can hear her, too. He's in his pen and he's looking this way. He looks wistful rather than keen. Oh, it's her, he seems to be thinking. Wonder what she wants.

At last she emerges from the office and Dora is behind her, pulling faces and rolling her eyes.

'Where's Mummy's darling, then?' she cries, suddenly all adoring and devoted and I wonder what on earth has come over her when I see Jack, our new kennel lad, heading our way with his muscles, wavy hair and tight shorts. Honestly, he's only eighteen, but that doesn't stop her having a good old gush for his benefit.

I fetch Kong and he yawns as she approaches. He gives her a polite wag of his tail and heaves a sigh. I long to wrap my arms round his huge neck and hug him goodbye, but I have to make do with a pat on the head. 'Bye Kong,' I say. 'See you soon.'

Gina gives me a steely look. 'You really should go on holiday, Maria,' she says. 'Somewhere hot and sunny.'

I'm not going to tell her I've been saving up for years for exactly that; my very own holiday of a lifetime. I've been saving up my time off as well, so I can make it a long one.

I'm on my way home from the travel agent's a few days later when the heavens open and several gallons of rain fall on my head. I hurry on, and have to pass Gina's huge house on my way. And there's Kong, tethered to a stake in the front garden.

He'll end up with rheumatism left outside in the wet like that. He looks as miserable as sin. So I rescue him. Well, what would you have done? I take him home, rub him dry with a couple of big colourful beach towels, and leave him to steam on the rug in front of the heater.

The phone rings and its Dora and she doesn't sound very happy. In fact, she is mad.

'Gina's just been here,' she says. 'Apparently she saw you making off with Kong. I managed to talk her out of calling the police.'

I look at Kong. He's on his back now, big grin on his face, legs up in the air. He's never looked so happy and here I am about to get the sack from the job I love. 'He was tied up outside in the rain,' I say in a small, apologetic voice.

'I know, she told me,' Dora goes on. 'Gina is pregnant and she says the smell of wet dog sets off her morning sickness.'

Oh, that makes it all right does it? 'Furthermore, his scratching is getting on her nerves, she's finding it much

60

too tiring to take him for walks and the muddy footprints are ruining her Axminster carpets.'

'Poor Gina,' I spit.

'Exactly,' Dora says, and I realise it isn't me she is mad with at all. 'I suggested that she should try to re-home him as her problems will only increase when the baby arrives.'

I sigh. If Kong is re-homed, then I may never see him again. The thought makes my heart ache.

'What did she say?'

'She said that he's a valuable dog and she's sure someone will be willing to pay a lot of money for him.'

I look at Kong. Kong looks at me. 'How much?' I ask, my stomach doing somersaults.

Dora gives a figure which is just about what I have saved for my holiday of a lifetime, the one I just booked at the travel agents.

Australia or Kong?

'Who wants to go to Australia anyway?'

'Well, actually,' Dora says. 'She doesn't want a penny. It's an easy solution for her. I was just making sure you really wanted him.'

Dear, sensible Dora. Boss in a million.

'Perfectly sure.'

'So you can still go to Australia and Kong can stay here until you get back,' she goes on. 'Reduced rates, of course.'

But I won't be going anywhere unless Kong can come with me. Australia is out. And Dora says I can bring him to work with me so he won't get lonely at home on his own. He'll like that – and so will I.

Edd Cross 2012

Make Like a Fishie

Pat Black

At first Marie thought she'd snagged the line on something in the water. A log, or a buoy perhaps. Then it gave
two sharp tugs. 'Oh, it… I think it's a fish!' She flinched
as the rod strained at an awkward angle, and the line
reeled out.

Stew, the American guy, was over in a flash.

'It might be a monster!'

'Hey! I've got a fish!'

Andy, Marie's husband, sat upright up his chair beside
the cabin, pulling off his sunglasses, 'Brilliant! Hey, we
won't go hungry tonight after all.'

Marie struggled to lift the rod and pull back like Captain José had shown her. The line continued to fizz out,
trailing a mini-wake of its own through the bright blue
water. 'It's heavy… Jesus!'

Stew grabbed the rod, helping Marie take the weight
of the fish. 'You sure ain't kidding, sweetheart. I think
you've got Moby Dick on the end of this.'

Andy grinned. 'You managing there, honey?'

'I think so… it's levelling out now.' The rod seemed
to thrum in her hands, like a twanged bow.

'That's awesome,' Stew's wife, Carla, called from her
own seat. 'Score one for the girls, lady!'

'I think this thing might end up scoring one for the
fishes,' Marie said. She cranked the rod, and this time the
line came in smoothly.

'You know how we used to catch fish back home, in
the canal?' Andy said to Stew. 'We used to reach right
into the water, and tickle them on the bum.'

'The what? On the bone?' Carla raised her sunglasses.

'Ah, no. *Bum.*'

'He means *tush*, sweetie,' Stew said. 'Well, if those are your tactics, you're welcome to try them on with this thing!'

Captain José appeared on deck; a short, bluff-looking man with a mass of white hair and a beard. Life at sea seemed to have given him a Hall of Mirrors bandy leggedness.

'You have fish, Señora?'

'Yes... it's giving me jip, José.'

'Jip?'

'I think she means *trouble*,' Stew said.

'Let me see...' José took the rod from Marie, and pulled hard on it. It bent again, spooling out yet more line. José uttered a quiet curse, and then called out for his First Mate, young Tony. 'Very, very big fish, Señora. You would like to try?'

'Well, yeah,' Marie said, taking the rod back once the line went straight again. 'I really didn't expect to land anything, though. What kind of fish do you think it is?'

'Shark,' said Stew. 'I'm betting on it.'

'It's big, whatever it is,' Captain José said. He peered over the edge, seemingly a little nervous about sticking his head too far over the transom. 'Very, very big.'

'Oh Christ, I don't want to catch a shark.'

Stew smirked. 'I wouldn't worry. They don't like being out of the water, you know.'

Suddenly Marie lurched forward as the rod almost pulled out of her hands. Andy was quickly there, an arm around her and a hand on the rod, keeping her steady. 'I think we're gonna need a bigger chip wrapper.'

'I'm not sure I want to catch this.' Marie laughed nervously, meeting her husband's eyes. 'What if it's the

64

Wrath of God?'

'Aw honey, sure you can catch it,' Carla said from her seat, sucking on a piña colada.

'Think about the story you'll have for when you get home.'

'Can anybody see it? That water's so clear, and it must be close.' Andy peered over, as unsure of himself as José had been.

Everyone, even Carla, came forward. The boat was being slowly buffeted on a gentle series of swells, out of sight of land.

'My arm's hurting,' Marie said. 'But it beats going to the gym, I suppose.'

'Keep in there,' Stew said. He patted her on the back. 'Hang on to it. That's a beast of a fish you got there, girl.'

'I think I saw something,' Tony the First Mate said, pointing. 'Over there.'

'I see it,' Andy said.

'Where?' Marie strained, the rod bent sharply.

'Just zipped past the boat,' her husband said. 'Very fast and very, very big.'

'Big, how?' Marie said. She felt a trickle of sweat travel down her left temple.

'Ah!' José exclaimed. He pointed off starboard, where the slick water seemed to boil and a flurry of bubbles spread over the surface.

'Marlin!' Tony cried, slapping both hands off the transom. 'A blue marlin. Santa Maria, look at it!'

The water frothed again, just in front of the boat now. The weight on the rod lessened, and Marie's hands felt curiously numb. Then the fish's dorsal fin breached, like a ragged tickertape streamer glinting in the sun. It was impossibly large. A tail followed it, smacking the surface

65

and showering the side of the boat.

'Oh my God,' Captain José said. 'The biggest I ever see.'

'I can't catch that,' Maria said. 'I can't lift that. I can't.'

'Good God, girl, you got lucky today,' Stew said. He raised his camera and clicked, clicked, clicked as the immense stiletto blade went deep with a flick of the tail.

José was shaking with excitement. 'At least twelve feet. At least!'

Andy breathed out, 'It's a whopper, darling. Well done!'

The shadow seemed to grow larger in the water. Carla shrieked, 'Oh my God, here it comes again!'

The fish leapt straight out of the sea, shaking its body from side to side. Its shiny black bill was pointed straight at them, bulbous eyes as big as cricket balls, the scales striped and purplish-blue, iridescent like the play of light on oil. It crashed back into the water, and they all flinched as the spray doused them. 'Why is it doing that?' Marie said, breathing hard.

'It's something to do with the hook you've put in its mouth,' Stew said. 'They jump out of the water to try and dislodge it. God damn, that's a fish and a half!'

'Fifteen feet,' Captain José said. 'Maybe more!'

'I don't want to catch it,' Marie said quietly. She turned to Andy.

'Maybe you should,' he said. 'Once in a lifetime thing, hon.'

'I don't want to.'

'You don't want to because you're scared, or you don't want to because you don't want to hurt it?'

'Both.'

'We've eaten a lot of fish suppers in our time. You

66

didn't feel bad about those.'

'I'll make a point of feeling bad about them when we get back to shore. Here.' Marie passed him the rod. Andy hesitated, so Stew stepped in. 'I'll take it if you guys don't want to do this. You could wait your whole damned life for a fish like that!'

'It is very valuable, also,' José said, soberly. 'It will bring a great price for its flesh.'

Marie bit her lip. Then the fish leapt out the water again, closer this time. She saw the muscle in its side tighten, the skin in between the spines of its dorsal fin contracting. 'I don't want to kill it. It's beautiful. It doesn't deserve it.'

Andy shrugged, 'I'm with you.' He indicated towards Stew, 'But Hemingway wants to have a pop.'

Stew was grinning. 'Alright, fish. Let's see what you've got.'

'Don't pull back so hard,' Captain José said. 'The rod wasn't made to take weight of a fish that size.'

'I know what I'm doing,' Stew said.

Andy gave Marie a hug. 'You alright?'

'It was like... I don't know... a prehistoric monster. The power in it. I've never seen anything like that. It's such a shame to kill it.'

'Remember what José said, hon. It's putting money in people's pockets. People who need it.'

'Here it comes!' Stew called out.

The marlin breached again, close enough to reach out and touch. And it kept on coming, desperately, pectoral fins trailing fine droplets of water, its belly stark white, rising straight and tall. Marie thought, no, you can't possibly be coming aboard? But that's exactly what the fish did. It cleared the transom, its shining thrashing bill narrowly missing everyone on board, and thwacked onto the deck. Then a blur of scales, Stew hauling on the rod despite his quarry being on board, Clara scuttling up the ladder towards the wheelhouse, Captain José with a billy club poised above his head.

Marie knelt down, avoiding the thrashing tail, reading something in those giant marble eyes. She reached towards the stark stripy belly near the anal fin. The fish jerked, coiled in on itself and then leapt off the deck. As it plunged back into the water, the line snapped with a flaccid sound like breaking of a guitar string.

Stew clung onto the rod, staring at the crazy pig's tail of twine dangling from it, mouth agape, and then closed, and then agape. You make like a fishie, Marie thought, staring out to sea, where the marlin had already disappeared completely from view.

Lucy Thornton 2012

New World

John Roberts

Everything had changed. This was dangerous. His fur flattened, ears lay back along his spine. The sun was coming through the clouds but it was quiet, no birds singing.

More important – the smells.

Not just wet grass and earth as it had been; now a chaos of other scents. Some he knew: pine sap, torn leaves, dead animal, but this wasn't the usual time for them. Other scents never smelled before. Could be anything. But strongest was the familiar odour of earth dug up from deep down.

No wonder. The ground was churned up with the roots of a tree sticking into the sky, the trunk no longer upright but lying on the ground just like they did after men had been. There could be anything crouching behind it now. All that had been familiar and safe here was different. Alien.

Nose twitching, he crept forward, alert. Here and there, untouched by what had happened, was something he recognised from before: a bramble, a rock, a tree stump, but that only made it worse, *more* different. He didn't want to go out, didn't want to be up here. Retreat back into the burrow. But he hadn't eaten for so long. Was it over now?

Cautiously, listening for any signs of movement, watching the sky for hawks, sniffing what was carried on the breeze, he moved out a little, trying to note the quickest route back. He couldn't rely on instinct, on his reflexes, to find his way.

Immediately ahead a tangle of branches blocked the trail. There was nothing for it but to lift his head above the trunk, sniff the air, listen, look all round before climbing up onto

71

the trunk and then sit up on haunches. Even from up here, he couldn't see far; more fallen trees everywhere, some of their branches pushed into the ground, other branches broken and sticking into the air like malformed limbs.

What was there to eat?

The edible plants near the burrow had been nibbled long ago. Must go farther afield. There, no way of knowing now where danger might be. There could be anything behind a trunk or the mess of branches at the end of it.

Beyond the edge of where the wood had been, out in the paddock, it didn't seem so bad. Rabbits he recognised from other burrows were feeding. But even here, the long coarse grass was flattened as if a horse had been rolling on its back.

He ran up the slope and looked around. It hadn't only been just near his own territory. Trees lay uprooted for as far as one could see. Back towards the conifer wood that had always been dark, so much sky was showing now. Beyond it a grassy hill was in view for the first time. Some trees hadn't fallen right to the ground but were leaning at awkward angles on others. A few were still upright, but those were dead and leafless.

He climbed over a slain conifer. No good bothering with that, the needles were bitter, without nutrition. But beyond it lay a fallen oak and now you could reach some of its leaves. Those which had been near the top were still green and succulent, not yet gone dry.

A squirrel was rooting around for acorns. Where would it live with the trees down? Where would the birds bring up their young next warm time? There were still hedgerows where smaller birds could nest but the bigger birds – owls, crows, magpies, and hawks – need tall trees.

A cock pheasant, bedraggled, with one or two tail feathers broken, was picking its way around a bramble

72

now spread even more widely than before. However had such a creature sheltered through the night? Good thing to have gone back to the burrow, not stayed living in the open. It had only been those rabbits who had stayed above ground, kept out of the warrens, who'd escaped the Great Illness of the past, seen the others' heads swell, watched them become lethargic and die in terrible pain. Now perhaps only those who had gone back to living underground survived this new disaster.

He'd known there was something else different this morning. There was not the occasional noise of those big roaring things that ran without legs along the long stretch of black stone and killed any creature in their path. Killed but didn't eat. Just left the dead rabbit, squirrel or pheasant mangled. With slow caution, keeping well clear of the fox trail, he made his way towards where the strange killers had always passed, leaving their acrid scent. No wonder there weren't any; fallen trees lay across the black stone. The things wouldn't be able to come through; they couldn't fly, could they? The thought of flying things made him look up. There hadn't been any of those creatures high up in the sky which made a droning noise, unlike birds, but didn't mean danger.

Turning back towards the paddock there was a small patch of young grass no-one else had found, and he stopped to feed. Farther out in the open, alone, a large buck was on the alert, would give a warning thump if anything approached. But if that happened, where to go from here? So many obvious ways had new obstacles, what had been the best hiding places were open and exposed now, offering no shelter.

Along the hedgerow there were new deep drifts of leaves, a blackbird turning them over in search of food. A poplar lay now stretching into the next field and had pushed down the wire net. He must be careful of that. Once, before the warm time, a badger had torn a hole in that net and when its scent had cleared some of them had gone through to where the earth was dug up and there were rows of plants not found out here: cabbages, sprouts and young broad beans with flowers. They had eaten well but when he had gone back next day there was a dead rabbit with a wire round its neck and later the hole filled again with wire netting.

Now, however, there was a great wide gap and rabbits in there already. While crossing the netting it was important to make sure claws didn't catch in it. Beyond it there were broad bean shoots, wonderfully sweet and tender. Next to them, poles that had stood in rows with plants twisted up them like bindweed lay broken and jumbled. Some had short round beans attached; in another pile were vines with longer flat green beans. The short round ones were tasty but the long ones, with delicious seeds inside, were even better. Another rabbit had sniffed out a row of carrots but they were small, shrivelled, with worms inside.

Just before the sun was at its highest the sound began in the distance – a rhythmic coughing like the badger made in its mating season but this had a screech which was painful to hear, and went on and on. Men were shouting amid the sound of wood crashing. It was to go on until the sun went down.

Worse was to come.

Sometime between sun's highest and twilight he first began to notice it, faint at first but growing stronger. There was no way of escaping it, even in the burrow. It came down there like a ferret would but even a ferret chased after only one at a time. This came to all creatures at the

74

same time, filled the nostrils until it was impossible to smell anything else, stinging and then making throat dry right down into the chest. The most dreadful. The most terrifying. The worst smell in the world: fire.

With it there was the noise of wood crackling sharply. For days it went on, with machines, men and fires growing closer, sparks rising up in the sky just the other side of the wood... what was left of it. Then, when the wind changed direction and the destroyers reached this edge of the wood, came the warmth. It was not a pleasant gentle warmth like that from the sun, which gave a sense of wellbeing in which many animals and birds would bask and doze, but a dry heat that made every creature feel unwell.

A few days later came rain, and relief. The fires went cold, the fresh smell of wet earth and grass returned. The men didn't come back, didn't bother with other trees which had fallen down outside the main wood. Near the roots those trunks were covered by hard thick bark with no goodness in it but at the end that had been high in the sky the bark was edible; would be useful in the cold time when the grass was covered with snow.

Meantime, he got used to the new way things were. Learnt that fallen trees were obstacles for predators, too. That grass and clover had been uncovered which would be useful now that all the beans and other plants near the fallen poplar, even the shrivelled carrots, were finished. Mapped the areas different animals were claiming, trying to build lives from ashes.

The secret to survival was to adapt to this new world.

Dan Widdowson 2012

Our Palm Civet

(*Paradoxurus Hermaphroditus*)

Hemal de Silva

We are urban dwellers and have been for many years. Our locality is about thirty-five kilometres from the capital Colombo, in Sri Lanka. About sixty years ago, when our parents were young and I was quite small, this region was completely different. It was a typical rural village, comprising mostly of small coconut and rubber plantations. On small farms, fruits and vegetables were grown on a commercial basis for the market in the capital. Low-lying areas were cultivated with rice, our staple diet. Poisonous and non-poisonous reptiles, amphibians and mammals lived in the area, and many kinds of birds, that either lived permanently or the migratory ones, visited us and all this was a joy to many and we did not feel bored living in a village.

It was a slow-moving and peaceful life. However, the peace and tranquillity in the region was often interrupted with problems that naturally occur in any type of society. Intoxication was one. Toddy, produced by tapping the unopened flowers of the Kitul Palm, was the common intoxicant and lead to domestic violence often.

Within one generation there was a complete change from the rural to a semi-urban and then an urban area. For many people it was a better life economically, but for some it was not such a positive change, with the village and the rural setting disappearing forever. The effect of the change in the environment was more pronounced for the populations of birds, bees, insects and animals.

For better or worse, we are now living in an urban area. The extent of land owned by individuals or a family

77

unit is small and restricted, but high in value. Living on small blocks of land like ours, means having neighbours close by, separated by parapet walls on the perimeter. Intoxication is now due to the consumption of more modern products; beer and arrack produced in factories. Addictions to drugs, harassing females who travel on lonely roads after work, snatching of necklaces, and stealing by organised gangs are now major problems.

What have all these normal activities of human beings in an urban neighbourhood to do with the Asian palm civet? They normally live in the wild where there are lots of trees, not in places densely populated with human beings. The ecological situation here at present is completely different to what it was before. With the migration of people in search of employment, better schools and medical facilities as well as higher incomes, the population shift to this area near the capital results in the demand for land for building blocks of ten to twenty perches of land.

A number of small green areas still remain in-between building projects, with many trees and small oases of forestland with coconut and other fruit trees, where the wild animals like the palm civet, bandicoot, mongoose and snakes still continue to breed and survive.

The sight of a cockroach and ants inside a house or a worm in a dug pit is considered distasteful. A harmless snake, a palm civet or a bandicoot are not or ever welcome. These animals are generally attacked when seen, or traps are set to catch them, or poisoned food kept to kill them when they have uprooted any plants or yams planted in the backyard or the little garden with the trimmed lawn is dirtied with the droppings of nocturnal visitors.

I was standing at the entrance to our compound one evening, resting my arms on the metal gate. It was evening, but not totally dark. As I was watching the moving vehicles on the tarred road, I saw an animal moving across the road about two hundred feet away, not really running, but walking briskly. At that distance I was not able to recognise the animal. It was about one and a half feet in length, eight inches in height and the fur probably brown in colour. There were no vehicles on the road now and this animal crossed the road safely. Possibly it knew exactly when to do it.

We live in an eleven perch block of land with the house taking about five and a half perches and the rest is the front and back yard. The house was built about fifty years ago. For some reason or another, there is a gap between the asbestos sheets and the roof beams, allowing animals to enter the space between the roof and the ceiling. Rats frequently move about in the ceiling. Rearing a female cat normally solves the problem of keeping the population of rats under control. As the space in the garden is restricted to a few perches, a dog has never been reared in our home.

In the night, we are used to one or two bandicoots running about in search of food and sometimes fighting with their mates. They have the habit of digging holes in the garden, especially where the soil is not compact and hard. The movements of a larger animal that made a different sound were heard now and then. One evening, as it was getting dark, I saw an animal about one and a half feet in length moving on the wall separating our compound with that of our neighbour. Judging by the size and the bushy tail, this animal appeared to be similar to the one I had seen crossing the road on that earlier occasion. It was bigger than a mongoose in size and may have been a racoon. The other option was that it was a palm civet.

This animal did not visit us every day but started doing it occasionally. As the distance between the wall and the rear of our roof is quite close it one day entered the space between the ceiling and the roof, making its characteristic noise. It appeared to be a pair judging from the noises made, and the visits and the sounds increased. The pair appeared to have decided to make this space above the ceiling their home. The two animals had probably mated. We expected the rat population to decrease now that we had other tenants in the ceiling. The nightly noises went on for some time and by then we had seen the animals in the garden as well and were certain that they were palm civets. The squeak of a young one was also heard.

One morning, working in the garden, I happened to look up. I saw a small brown head with two bright eyes and small ears watching me without moving, peeping from between the roof and the beam of the wall. I was excited to see this little animal, watching me quite unafraid. It did not move at all but continued to look directly at me. The look indicated curiosity and the animal did not appear to be frightened at all to see me below. The head, ears and the snout were brown in colour; the nose at the tip of the snout was black. I could not see the body of the animal, but from the small size of the head it had to be an immature civet. This probably was the first time this baby civet had seen a human being. Was the baby civet trying to recognise the big animal down below? The look of the baby civet clearly showed that it was not afraid to continue to watch me. I too watched, just as fascinated. I did not wish to call my wife and daughter to take a look at this baby civet as it would have caused it to disappear immediately. Maybe it suddenly decided I was dangerous or had inspected me thoroughly enough, as it turned and disappeared without a noise.

Ultimately, the noises and the movements of the civet family stopped suddenly. They had moved away unannounced and as suddenly as they had arrived. Were they being good quests who did not wish to out-stay their welcome?

Occasionally, the presence of civets in the garden was confirmed from their usual noise of fighting and moving about in the backyard. When the light on the outside wall was switched on it was possible to see the animals, often a pair but on one occasion there were three civets prowling around. Occasionally, it was possible to watch the mature civets closely, though they never did linger to be observed for a long time. Maybe for a minute or two they continued to roam in the garden after the light was switched on, but then would quickly disappear. Three rows of dark lines on the top of the body were quite noticeable. Switching on the light did not scare them away immediately and the animals would look up for just a little while then continue with searching for food, sniffing with their noses close to the ground. They may not have been frightened as they were, by then, used to the surroundings and had not encountered any predators. We started noticing palm seed, germinated ones and seedlings with just one leaf above the ground. There must have been a tree or two close by. Though civets are fond of the toddy, this would not have been available in the vicinity. It was possible that they had transported the palm seeds to our garden as they liked to feed on ripe berries!

It was from a news story on the Al Jazeera TV channel that I first heard about Kopi Luwak. In Indonesia, where

81

coffee is grown extensively, a new small scale agro industry has evolved thanks to the palm civet. In the coffee growing areas people living in villages are collecting the droppings of palm civets to extract the undigested and intact coffee seeds from them. The people are said to travel long distances in search of the droppings, starting their work early in the morning. The seeds are separated from the collected droppings, washed and given a thorough cleaning and dried. The skin of the berry did not adhere to the seeds and they were undamaged. These particular seeds fetch high prices. This only takes place when the coffee trees have ripe berries. The seeds thus collected, when roasted and ground produce a superior cup of coffee, with a nutty flavour, favoured by connoisseur coffee drinkers willing and able to pay the high price of the seed or the brewed coffee. There is a good demand for the seed and the coffee in Western countries. The price remains high as the supply is limited. The process and collection method obviously does not matter!

It is especially in Indonesia that the villagers are collecting these coffee seeds with a unique flavour. It can happen if palm civets live in coffee growing areas. As the name signifies, the Asian palm civet is a common animal in the region. The civet is said to feed on the best ripened coffee berries during the night, when they normally go in search of food, and the droppings have to be collected the next morning.

Research carried out has shown that the seed, once swallowed, is not damaged in any way and the intact seeds pass with the animal's droppings, but a chemical process that occurs during the passage of the seed through the civet's stomach 'treats' the seed, giving the unique flavour to it. While the palm civet does the unique processing free of charge, do the collectors, agents, processors and those who enjoy the cup of coffee give any thought or thanks the palm civet? I hope at least in Indonesia, the palm civet is held in high esteem.

This was an interesting bit of news to me and I lost no time checking the web for more information. There was information about Kopi Luwak but not so much of what happens while the coffee seeds pass through the alimentary canal of the civet. There is a good demand for the special coffee and the price is extraordinarily high. I knew the palm civet was a well-known animal in Sri Lanka, coffee is grown in the country, and at least two civets visited my garden occasionally... so...

I was not willing to forget this matter due to the unique natural method of producing a superior grade of coffee in such high demand. Also, this product is organic, in fact! With difficulty, I was able to obtain a couple of small trees in polythene bags. It was a hybrid variety, and the two small trees had remained unsold in a nursery.

I devised a method to produce Kopi Luwak. As I knew two palm civets visited our garden, albeit occasionally, I planted the two coffee plants in our garden. The existing berries were wasted and I hopefully waited for the next season. During this intervening period the civets visited our garden on several occasions, judging by the noises they made. Finally, there were flowers, then berries and they started to ripen. Several days later, one morning it was clear that the ripe berries had been eaten the previous night. As the sound of civets moving about was also heard, I was certain that they had fed on the ripe coffee berries. The search began for the droppings. Within our garden it was nowhere to be found. A few days later the civets were heard moving about and more ripe berries had disappeared by morning. Once again a good search was made, but there were no droppings. The long awaited opportunity to taste the special coffee never materialised!

Only a human being could have done that.

We felt a little sad to see it lying there. This may have been the same civet I had watched several times and listened to its movements and fighting in the garden on many occasions. It may have been the same civet that had fed on the ripe coffee berries and made me search for the droppings. Was it the baby civet who had watched me with such curiosity and without any fear? I had no answer to these questions. There was only one thing left for us to do.

I dug a pit deep and long enough to bury the animal. With a mamoty I lifted the palm civet and laid it gently at the bottom of the pit. After closing the pit with the excavated earth, my wife and I placed a heavy stone on the grave so that no other animal would get the opportunity to dig at that spot. We could only give our palm civet a decent burial.

The civets continued to visit our garden occasionally and were not troublesome at all. Now and then I used to switch on the garden light to see them moving about and leaving soon after. One morning, my wife called me hysterically and told me to take a look in the backyard. A mature civet lay dead. We watched the dead animal for a little while, then touching it realised that it was stiff. The carcass was on a rock with the head resting on the ground and the rest of the stiff body lying at an angle of about twenty-five degrees. I noticed a little blood on the side of the snout. One eye was open. It was obvious the civet had died some hours ago. The carcass was not hugging the contour of the rock. This would have been the case if it had died at that spot. There was no possibility of the stiff body falling from the roof above to land where the animal was laying. I suspected that the dead civet had been thrown over the wall.

Dan Widdowson 2012

The Princess and the Porker

Madeleine Sara

Dainty mouthfuls through missing teeth and aging gums prolong the mealtimes of our more senior cat, while a bubble of saliva escapes her lip when she's contented. At the age of eleven years, Tarragon is still our beautiful Princess with marmalade fur. She's the kind of cat who sits, head held high, waiting for us to dance attendance to her. She may, if we are especially good, deign to grace us with her presence and might even condescend to grant cuddles and stroking. She's perfectly regal. Sadly, her Prince Consort, Comfrey, had recently died at the age of almost eighteen years and is greatly missed by us all.

Poor Tarragon, lonely and miserable, needed a new companion. After a few weeks of mourning we decided to contact our local Cats Protection. Buoyed up by our previous successes at integrating new members into our feline family, and confident that Tarragon would know how to share her home, Borage became our fourth protégé. At sixteen weeks he was congenial and benevolent, comically cute with a penchant for dripping taps and swirling bath water. He trilled contentedly and being a black and white, semi-long haired Tom, we wondered whether he might have Maine Coon ancestors. To our complete dismay, however, Tarragon was unimpressed and when Borage came within a whisker's length, her feline admonishments would turn the air blue; she made it quite clear he was not welcome.

Un-phased by Her Royal Highness, Borage got on with settling in. He adopted a philosophical approach to his new companion, reflected in his unquashable enthusiasm. On my return from the supermarket he would run excitedly to greet me with a cheerful trilling mew that cracked silly smiles across my face. He would then leap in and out of the vast hessian shopping bags that covered the kitchen floor.

Having emptied one shopping bag, I tossed one of his toys inside it. His expression became manic and his eyes flared with excitement as he pounced and rummaged.

Eventually his crazy antics unearthed the fluffy pom-pom from the bag, making him race around the kitchen floor like David Beckham across a football pitch. I am impressed by his footwork and his speed, dribbling and tossing the pom-pom with complete focus. Tarragon, meanwhile, remained on her cushion, relieved that the shopping bag and the action were sufficiently far away not to bother her rest; although her composure was periodically disrupted by a wary surveillance through half-opened eyelids.

Being a Princess, naturally she has a most discerning palate, while Borage will eat just about anything. That of course became the problem. He'd suck up his portion of cat food and then hurry off to find her, quietly and painstakingly munching. Paralysed with horror, Tarragon would watch in meek, stunned silence as this young male interloper would appear from nowhere to suck up her meal like a high-powered vacuum cleaner. She'd hiss, spit and swipe at him. Then she'd snarl and scratch at us for good measure, complaining if we so much as touched her, after all it was our fault.

It wasn't as if their bowls were side by side. They weren't even fed in the same room. Tarragon dined on the countertop in the utility, while Borage ate on a tray on the kitchen floor. We only needed to turn our backs for a second and he'd execute the deed with daredevil aplomb. Shouting and removing him from the area seemed to do little to deter his dogged determination.

While Tarragon became thin, withdrawn and constipated, Borage's little body swelled like a Conference Pear on legs. The extra protein made him hyperactive and destructive so that he would chew parcels left by the front door for posting, shred the leaves on the Christmas Cactus and gnaw at the cables for the mobile charger.

Things had to change.

We started shutting Tarragon in while she ate, busying ourselves with chores until we would suddenly remember our poor exiled Princess, shut in alone with only the washing machine and tumble dryer for company.

Watching Cesar Millan, the *Dog Whisperer*, on TV prompted me to change the way I managed Borage's mealtime raids. I knew I had to be hands-on and persistent. No slacking, no wavering and no shouting. Previously we had fed Borage first, thinking to distract him while we then fed Tarragon, but that just meant he'd had a head start. I began to prepare her meal first, giving him kibble second, and then positioning myself beside her on sentry duty while she ate. As soon as Borage jumped up onto her countertop he would receive a small poke in his flank that broke his blinkered concentration. Then he was made to jump down, so that the maximum effort he exerted gave him minimum rewards. The feline *'tss'* sounds I made to accompany this action also warned him away. By the end of a week the message began to sink in; I only needed to '*tss*' if he so much as looked up at her countertop and he'd scoot outside, leaving her in peace.

Borage became much calmer; plants and parcels were no longer torn to shreds and Tarragon began to enjoy mealtimes, unmolested. She would again raise her head up to my hand to be stroked. Harmony reigned once more.

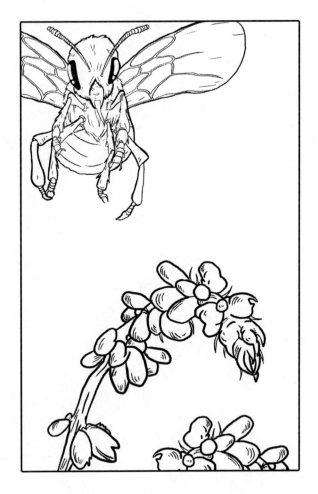

Dan Widdowson 2012

Queen Bee

Jennifer Domingo

Heat pierces my body and floods my insides. I feel the warmth spread into my wings. They shudder alive and unfurl from their tight knot on my back. I can feel them quiver, I can feel them stretch and ache for the brightness. As I gulp my first breath of air, I feel them taut and eager to move. They are impatient to go and I surrender to them as they lift me up, up, up into a vast canvas of blues and yellows and purples and greens. Oh the smells, they shout at me from all sides, confusing me, pulling me here and there and only the rhythmic beating of my wings keeps me sane. The air is heady with aromas – sweet, pungent, bitter, sour – all so new and different, and yet so familiar, even if I cannot recall a time before. I only know of now. I only know I need to act fast before the warmth disappears, before my insides turn cold again and my wings shatter.

Wispy trails of edible odours zigzag across the air. I latch onto one of them. It promises nourishment, but there is something tagging along with it I do not recognise, mingling with the ripe promise. My wings beat faster in panic. I hear my throat vibrate, drawing out my poison. This unknown entity drags me to where my food is. I must go to this monster and get past it if I am to feed. My hunger drives me. I know my anxiety echoes much too loudly and my wings try to hush the noise. I move onwards, forwards towards the sea of green with splashes of brown, smudges of amber and splodges of earth. I see my banquet of yellow buds bursting with sweetness, promising me nourishment.

I also see the monster giving off aromas unlike any other. They confuse me. The monster is covered in something I cannot explain. The shape is unrecognisable. The monster moves very, very slowly and lumbers on – big and lumpy and in the way of my yellow buds. What type of beast is this? It's just there, smelling of nothing I know, coloured in nothing I understand, sending up trails of mud and ice and death. My fear makes me want to pull away but I cannot; I must eat, I must feed. The monster casts a long, dark shadow. I must keep away from its darkness. I need the light. I must stay in the light. I cannot get cold.

I move around the monster. My wings take me high and around. Its shadow darkens the air, dark like in my cocoon before the warmth woke me and imbued me with strength. The monster draws the heat away with its presence. It is much too powerful. It echoes louder than my fear. But for a moment my wings slow down. I drop. I glide under the monster's shadow and straight to one of the yellow buds. Its soft petals are still shut tight. I tear at it to get to the sweetness. The shadow seems far, far away. Now there is only the rush of sugar-sweet syrup. I drink, I feast. I am covered in the bud's dust. I feel my insides quiver. I feel something stir. My precious larvae are awake. They spur me further on to the next bud, then the next and then another. I tear at the yellow petals, gorging on their sweetness. Their dust coats me and weighs me down, but I continue. I must feed. They must feed.

The monster is never far away. I move as fast as I can. My wings tire from the weight of the dust. I rip through one more bud and I eat and then I'm off, satiated, heavier and warmer.

My larvae are eager to burst forth. My wings know where to take me. I follow a trail. I know this trail. It calls to me

94

as the warmth did, as the sweetness did. I know I need to be there. But then it stops. The trail ends in nothingness. Something has removed it. After a certain distance, I cannot sense it anymore. Fear returns. It growls louder than before. Suddenly out of the gloom the monster reappears. My larvae scream and I attack.

The shadow moves away and I feel a rush of air as it coaxes me along and into a crevice. The shadow disappears as I am enclosed in a different cocoon, a solid one. I smell new wood. I settle down on some moss and the new aromas overwhelm. Moss feels soft as the yellow petals. I walk around, feel the warmth and taste the scent of newness. I do not know where I am but my wings have settled down and my larvae have stopped screaming.

The monster's shadow passes along the entrance of my new den but it no longer matters. I have much work to do; I have an empire to build and my babies will need a strong hive.

Mortimer Sparrow 2012

Mortimer

Mortimer Sparrow

Do you believe in destiny?

Life has certainly made me a more cynical person as I have grown and realised that the world is not that fairy-tale place I had hoped for, and yet, when I am asked this question, the corners of my mouth curl into a smile. I cast my mind back to the day that I met my true love and my life changed forever. At the time of writing this, I have been blessed for over seven years with the company of the most passionate of little loves, who is happy to see me every day, who trusts me completely and who has been my constant in a changing life and world.

Once upon a time, about seven years ago at the beginning of July, the sky was open and blue, everything seemed greener outside and the birds were darting around into the trees and hedgerows surrounding the cottage. My sister and I were watching a mouse (that she had named Herman) sitting outside his mouse hole in the grass, eating some seed. We heard the tiniest, barely audible sound of something cheeping or beeping; we followed the sound with our eyes up to the corner of our cottage and in the old stone work, right at the top; there was a hole with something sticking out of it. That insignificant little pink thing that would change my world was the tiny, naked head of a little baby bird. The sun was pounding down, straight onto it, but the hole in the wall was much too high up to do anything. My sister left a thick jumper directly below, just in case the little beeping jelly bean should fall.

My next memory is of me sat in the house and my sister

running in very upset. 'The baby fell and it is dead.' My sister cried and I went over to her to hug her. Then the door opened; it was my father, 'He is alive, but we have to be quick.' He opened his hands that seemed huge to reveal the tiny pink clean jelly bean in the middle of his soil and grass stained gardening gloves.

I remember the sense of responsibility, the instant maturing, that scared feeling of being responsible for something so delicate and fragile. I remember that she had my heart as soon as I saw her.

We found out what to feed her by looking on the Internet (thank you, Internet, I love you!) and also found out that she was a day old. Examination of the birds flying into the nest confirmed that she was a little house sparrow. I knew nothing of rearing any animal but I threw myself into it. I remember that first morning; I fell asleep sat upright holding a little bowl with her safely cushioned in it.

I had a lovely boss and worked in a small new age shop. I used to take her in her bowl in a wicker basket with a hot water bottle and all of her food for the day. I kept her behind the counter with me.

I stared at her all of the time, fascinated and somehow horrified that I could see and sometimes hear her little insides working away. Then one day, she looked at me. A tiny black dot appeared in the centres of her blind eyelids and then they both slowly opened and we just stared at each other. Her eyes were so pure, so clean and sparkling, they could finally put a face to the voice that had been shepherding her all over the place and talking to her about everything.

After meeting my little sparrow I developed tunnel vision; the most important thing was getting her strong and feathered. I always thought she was a boy and I named her Mortimer – it simply suited the naked jelly bean so well. She steadily grew her feathers and was a beautiful girl; but no matter, her name was still Mort.

Getting to know Mortimer certainly broadened my horizons and my sister's; I have always been anti-animal cruelty but I ate animals. This contradiction became glaring. Learning how much intelligence, awareness and love a little bird has really made me aware of something that should be obvious, but masked over as being the 'norm' – we should not deny any kind of 'jelly bean' the chance to grow and live a life. They should never know fear at human hands. My sister and I started off as a vegetarian and then became vegan after looking into the reality of factory farmed animals. I was, and am still, horrified. Mort lives off a vegan diet and she can recommend it, too.

In terms of action, Mort inspired me to go beyond just changing my diet and lifestyle. I see things for what they are now and understand that shooting and hunting is as low as the people slitting throats in the abattoirs. I was young when I fell in love with my little sparrow teacher and I can't remember everything, but I remember some things very vividly, like putting on my camouflage gear, wading through a stream, and crawling across a corn field to a secret pheasant rearing pen. It was empty at that time but all around the edges there were traps and dead animals strung up by their necks, nailed onto posts; typical game keeper decoration. There was squirrels, weasels, stoats, rabbits and maybe other animals, but some were so rotten I could not tell what they had been. Others had clearly just been taken out of traps that day. I cut them all down. I set off all of the hidden traps and threw them into the river. I cut the wire fence open. I tipped the strategically placed feeders into the river; they encourage animals to stay close by, so that when the shooters arrive they don't have to look too far for something to murder.

There was plenty of food in my garden a little while away; I thought I would give these animals a chance, no matter how small. I was in a bit of a rage actually; it disgusted me. We had made friends with a pheasant at our home; we called him Scratch because he had a scar across his face. He used to run down the field when we called him and ate from our hands. One day he stopped coming and I knew in my heart that it was not because he had found a mate and gone off somewhere to be happy. Scratch did not just leave me with photographs of us together, he left me with the knowledge of how gentle these animals are, and I will never stop defending them.

We also took a large cage from that horrible enclosure, which would later be a temporary home to a duck recovering from a broken wing.

Puddlebum was a completely wild duck who was all alone on a small pond in the middle of the countryside. Every afternoon we would go to the back door and shout her name, and she would respond from the other side of a field and trees and come running up the garden. One day she went missing and returned with a broken wing. We had to catch her and get it bandaged. At first she was scared of us but ended up lying on us and chasing us around the garden... and it was not for food, it was because she wanted to... for fun! As her wing would never heal properly and we did not have a pond we, took her to a farm sanctuary. The last time we visited she had paired up with a male mallard.

There have been so many animals' lives that we have tried to help because of Mort; she taught us to see the birds and the other animals. I seemed to be finding so many so I wanted to learn more about how to treat injuries and illnesses. I applied to be a volunteer in a wildlife rescue that was about twenty miles or so away from me. Everything was going great at the meeting with the owner until I mentioned Mort.

'You are breaking the law by keeping her and she must be miserable in a cage; you have to do what is right for her. We will release her from here with others. I can put Tippex on her head so that you know which one is her.'

As if I would need the Tippex.

I did take her outside when she was younger; I probably should not have because it was a completely foreign world to her. I opened my hands and she flew off, startled. She went in a straight line to the end of the very large garden, which was completely open in the countryside. 'Was that Mort?' My father asked from the other side of the garden. I replied that it was and then he said he would have liked to have said Goodbye.

I ran off down the garden, realising that I had made a stupid mistake and I started to panic. I called her when I had reached the large tree at the end of the garden, and she came charging out of the tree chirruping loudly, telling me off. I put my cupped hand in my jumper sleeve as I always do and she ran in there and did not come back out until I was in the house.

I walked into the house and heard my father telling my mother 'Mort has gone, she flew away.' I opened the door and looked at them and Mort jumped out from my jumper and hopped up on my shoulder.

Phew! Fancy thinking a imprinted, tame and happy bird would know what to do in the wild... this brings me back to that wildlife rescue; I waited a couple of years and then I tried again. I changed my hair a lot and guessed that the old woman might not notice I was the 'law-breaking sparrow torturer'. The lady did not remember me. I decided to put that upsetting accusation behind me because I genuinely wanted to help animals and there was nowhere closer. I learned quite a lot there and most importantly I became confident with handling different animals and finding out what was wrong with them.

One day a member of staff from there told me something ; it was the owner's policy to put very young baby birds to sleep as they were 'a lot of trouble and don't often survive.' I said that I would take any home and rear them for release, but to no avail.

Of course I cast my mind back a few years to Mort's first days, she was lucky to make it, but I knew nothing about birds and had no equipment when I raised her and yet these people would not even give the little ones a chance. I imagined Mort's soft skin being pierced by a needle and her life being taken away from her when there was nothing wrong with her. I felt sick and let down and I did not want anything more to do with a place that gave up on something before they had even tried. If I had taken Mort there when I had found her, they would have killed her. I never went back.

Mort lives with me on the opposite side of the country to where we started out seven years ago. We have lived in five different houses, I have had five different jobs and she has stuck with me and has always been happy as long as I have. There have been times in my life when things have been difficult – that is life – but when my eyelids close I imagine Mort kicking her legs, scooting across the material on my jumper or the bed and I am reminded that there is beauty, purity and hope in the world.

Working for other people is something that I have never liked; it has always seemed incredibly stupid that someone will pay me pieces of paper and metal for hours of my life that I will never get back. The problem became worse when I met Mort as I always wanted to be with her. I have lost jobs, quit jobs and given up jobs to be with her. Happily, I am in a position now where I am working from home and I can be with her all of the time. Maybe I am a bit of a hermit, but I challenge you to find someone quite so contented as I am.

There is a lot to tell but not enough time to tell it I am afraid. We have made so many new animal friends; I now take birds into my home and look after them or raise them before they are released into the wild. We have four ex-battery cage hens that I am absolutely in love with, that my partner and I rescued from a re-homing day; the state they were in was terrible but they live a life under the clouds now.

I would like to think of myself as an activist. I greatly admire people who stand between the bullies and the bullied. Why wouldn't I want to be one of those people? If life were a fairy tale I like to think that I would be a goodie, with a fairy on my shoulder, defending the defenceless from the monsters. Even if it might not end in happily ever after, I close my eyes and see that little chest rising and falling with the most steadfast and pure little heartbeat and those shining brown eyes and I find it impossible to believe that this life and this world is meant to be anything less than wonderful and beautiful for every creature.

At the very least, as humans we have the ability to help it to be fair for every creature.

I have always lived with my younger sister and she has always been my best friend. She loves Mort like I do and Mort loves her. We rescue animals together. We defend the defenceless together. Let us not forget who put that jumper down that saved Mort's life. This story is dedicated to her and Mortimer; my triangle.

Painted by Rosie's rescuer, Elizabeth C. Koubena

Rosie Roadrunner

Elizabeth C. Koubena

When I first saw Rosie, she was running across the yard at the Society for the Protection of Stray Animals Wildlife Hospital on the island of Aegina, her two front legs dragging her whole body. She looked up at me and grabbed my heart. You know how it happens. Sometimes you meet an animal that you instantly bond with. So it was with Rosie and I.

I resisted taking her home that first day because we had so many other cats. The next day, however, I found out about her situation. She had been hit by a car, they told me, and someone had picked her up and brought her to the wild animal clinic. They were giving her vitamin B injections with the hope that it would help regenerate her damaged spinal cord. But they weren't very hopeful. Since they were overloaded with animals, I understood that despite their best intentions, Rosie would probably not get all the care she needed. I had to bring her home.

She settled in immediately and we began her therapy: vitamin B, massage baths, physiotherapy on her hind legs, plus the obvious good food, a warm place to sleep and lots of hugs.

Despite her lower body paralysis, Rosie got around amazingly fast. That's how she got her name – Rosie Roadrunner. She was first at the dinner table, first up a tree, she chased the others through the grass; she seemed completely oblivious of her handicap. She was a happy, easy-going cat and got along with everybody.

Some of the nerves in Rosie's lower body did come back to life, but unfortunately they had a mind of their own and

107

Rosie couldn't control them. Nor could she control her urine. I gave her medicated baths to calm her irritated skin and cleaned her every day.

Nursing Rosie, I was filled with admiration for the way she accepted her discomfort, for the stoicism she exhibited during treatment, for her acceptance of an imposed physical limitation and finally, I stood in awe of her acceptance of death. When her kidneys began to fail, she wanted to lie by the warm radiator in our kitchen more and more. She stopped climbing trees, stopped playing with the other cats, and then one day, she stopped eating. I bathed her and dried her and made her comfortable in the basket and offered her some food. She looked at me with a serious, wise look and then closed her eyes.

In a country like Greece, overflowing with so many strays, the weak and sick animals don't often get the care they need. 'It's the survival of the fittest', you hear people say. Rosie forced me to reconsider this idea. Though weak in body, she was strong in spirit and she taught me so much.

She gave me a great gift when she died. You might find what I am about to tell you hard to believe, but it did happen. Rosie was in a coma and near death; I was holding her cuddled in a blanket in my arms and suddenly, an image jumped into my head. Rosie was standing at the edge of a field. She looked straight into my eyes, and then turned and ran on all four legs into the tall green grass.

Mortimer Sparrow 2012

Terrorists on Horseback

Jenny Elliott-Bennett

Heat evaporates the scent. If there is no scent, then there is nothing for the hounds to follow. This is why fox hunting season runs from August to March; in colder weather the scent literally lays on the ground, chilled still.

At ten o'clock the aged and scarred Landrover pulled up at the train station. Here it picked up sabs that had come from all directions across the south. Bundled into the back, spirits were high as maps and bottles of citronella spray were handed out, camcorders and radios checked, and spare gloves, jackets and compasses were shared.

As we drove to the meet, the Commander gave us a run-down of tactics for the day. From his shot gun position, he pivoted around and looked at his troops in the back of the truck, our love and respect for him enhanced by his paternal concerns, 'OK, children, locate the meet point on your maps – Warren Lodge, Shakleford. Look to the right; see Sheephatch copse? That is part of Moor Park Nature Reserve; if you can get footage of them in there, we can report them. Not many roads in this area, so it will be hard to move you about. Gonna be a hard day's running, children.'

We like to get to the meet in plenty of time before the hunt set off, which is usually at eleven. The Commander has spies everywhere, which is how we know when and where the meets are. Meets used to be advertised in magazines like *Horse and Hound*, but hunts have stopped publicly advertising because what they do is illegal and they don't want to let sabs or police know when and where they will be out. We can't use details of every meet; last minute ones can't be sabbed because it might blow

111

our moles. When we are going to attend, we inform the police. It is good for us if they are there, as it means the hunt can't get really violent. When the police don't show, or go home early, human blood spills.

Whilst the gathered hunters were swigging port and smoking on horseback, we orientated ourselves; we sighted the public footpaths and bridle paths, looked on the map to see the possible directions the hunt could go in, and provisionally planned what our tactical response would be for each possible direction.

The longer they spend at the meet drinking and laughing, the better; if it takes them half an hour to set off, then that is half an hour extra that the foxes have to themselves, and half an hour less that we have to try to keep up with horses.

The hunt master called order and welcomed the riders, all of whom pay a cap fee to go on these hunts. Sometimes he explains who we, the group of horse-less bystanders dressed in black, are – 'Don't worry about the saboteurs, they won't ruin our fun! Just a lot of jobless townies!'

And then they were off. At speed. Thirty-odd blood-thirsty terrorists on horseback, galloping north uphill, followed by a pack of forty hounds and three quad bikes. The terrier men drive these bikes and the terrier dogs are in wooden crates on the front of the bikes.

There are no public rights of way headed north. That is why the hunt chose to go in that direction. The map showed a byway crossing a mile beyond the hill they were going up, so we were back in the truck to get to that byway via the only proper road in the district. We got out half way along the byway to listen. We heard the convoy of hunt support vehicles approaching. They appeared, and we watched them turn into a field. They surrounded the small copse at the foot of Stone Hill. We saw flashes of redcoats and white hounds in the trees. They were drawing the wood. This is the process of systematically putting hounds in to search for foxes.

We were stuck on the byway, quarter of a mile away from the hunt; we couldn't follow them in as the police were standing with us. The hunt were on private land, so if we made a wrong move we would likely have been arrested for trespassing. We could only film proceedings from our vantage point. A few hounds started whining; they had a scent. We looked at the policemen; we didn't know these ones and so we didn't know how far we could push it before they arrested us.

'You can't expect us to just stand here and watch them rip a fox apart.'

'We don't care about the foxes, and anyway, ones you save today will only get killed tomorrow; we are here to prevent a breach of the peace. If you leave this byway, you are trespassing.'

'They are illegally hunting.'

'No they are not, they are laying a trail. They told us they would be laying trails all day.'

'Of course they told you that, but if they were really only trail hunting, they wouldn't need to bring the small terrier dogs out with them, which are put down the fox holes. Do you get it?'

The policeman shrugged his shoulders.

'Oh, you must be one of the coppers that they pay off. They have told us all about it; they boast that they have got a few of you firmly in their pockets.'

No response.

The hounds got louder. The sabs all grouped together. If you were spread out and a fox ran out, it would turn back on seeing a staggered line of humans and you were in danger of scaring it back in the direction of the hounds. Huddled together, we made a small unit that a fox would feel comfortable running past without veering off its escape course. 'Hounds, hounds!' we called out in unison as loudly as we could, keeping our voices deep to mimic the hunt staff commands. We called repeatedly for ten seconds. One by one the hounds started to run out of the copse and across the grass towards us, tails wagging, ears pricked. We brought the whole pack to us in this way. 'Good doggies, good doggies!'

The red coats came thundering out of the trees to us.

'Shut the fuck up you idiots!'

I looked at the policeman standing next to me, 'Nice bunch, aren't they?'

The hunt master started on the copper, 'You can't be fucking serious; you just let them call our hounds? They are not allowed to do that!'

The policemen conferred. We were told the verdict, 'You can't disrupt a lawful activity.'

'Prove that it is lawful.'

'They are only trail hunting.'

'So they say, but we know from experience with this hunt that that is a lie. We sab them up to three times a week; we know what they do.'

'Well, as far as we can see, they are only trail hunting, so you can not disrupt that.'

'The hunt master does not have control of his hounds. Look how easily we took them off him! He is running around with a pack of hounds he can't control. What about public safety?'

The policemen looked unsure. The hunt master piped up, 'We are on private land; there is no 'public safety' on private land.'

The entire hunt were gathered at the edge of the field by this point; hounds, horses, quads. Suited us; while they stand around arguing, foxes escape. Another red coat started, 'Call yourselves fucking animal lovers? You are confusing the hounds! Stop messing with their minds!'

We have heard some stupid shit out of these people's mouths, but this was incredulous. We retorted, 'Better a confused hound than a murdered fox!'

The hunt moved off slowly, heading east. Half of us followed along beside them on the byway, whilst the other half got back into the truck, to circumnavigate the private land on the only tarmacked road and be dropped off in front of the hunt about a mile or so ahead, at the entrance to a bridle path. Most of the coppers got in their 4x4s and followed our truck. The horses started to canter, and we ran along with two policemen trying to keep pace behind us. The hunt came out of the field and crossed the byway to take up a footpath. We consulted maps and compass and radioed the Commander, 'Hunt heading south-east on the footpath that comes out at Lockley Farm.'

'OK, I will put foot sabs in at the other end of that footpath. There is a copse behind the farm – it is private but has a few public paths going through it. Be prepared to get in there. It is very hilly, so they will try to lose you over the hard terrain.'

'Copy that.'

We ran down the footpath. We discovered the terrier men half a mile in, parked up on their quads. We filmed them blocking the public footpath with their vehicles; another clip to send to Surrey County Council. We waited with the quads until the two policemen had caught up with us, 'Look, they are blocking this public right of way and you are not allowed motorised vehicles on footpaths.'

The police questioned the terrier men, 'What are you doing?'

'Just having a rest.'

'You are blocking the footpath.'

With this, they pulled off the footpath into the woods, about two feet from where they had been. They turned off the engines and grinned at us. The terrier dogs were whimpering in their wooden boxes. The coffin-like crates have no windows cut out of them, only a few very small air holes drilled down the side. We could see little claws being pushed through the air holes, and heard frantic scraping and pitiful whimpering.

Suddenly the hounds were in cry. I looked at the sab nearest to me; the desperate anxiety in her eyes and the panicked expression on her face mirrored mine. We radioed, 'Hounds in cry in forest that is shown on the right of the footpath that leads from the byway to Lockley Farm.'

The Commander came back, 'OK, more foot sabs coming in from the south, should be with you in five minutes.'

We sprinted a few hundred yards further along the path to get away from the cops, and dived into the forest. We charged forward up a steep gradient, the thigh-high brambles tearing skin through our trousers and the dense branches scratching our faces. We were upon the pack; they were circling a large briar patch, screaming. Most of the dogs were fighting their way through the thick bracken, inching further and further into the patch, getting nearer and nearer to the fox. Our low and loud voices resonated through the trees, 'Leave it! Leave it!' We were pushing hounds away out of the edges of the briar patch. They were so delirious to be on scent that it was hard to get their attention. They didn't notice as the brambles drew blood from their snouts and chests. We sprayed citronella all over the brambles to mask the scent, all the while pushing hounds away and calling commands with voices ever raspier. Time seemed to slow. The narrative in my head was loud; move forward, spray that area. I looked down and watched my right knee come up and my leg stretch over a fallen tree trunk. My right arm came forward and I sprayed, whilst I held the camera up in my left hand. There was a flash of auburn in the brambles. We dived forward, spraying the fox's path, under the noses of the hounds, struggling through the heavy brush, all the time bellowing 'Leave it! Leave it!' It was chaotic. There were hounds everywhere. We fought on like this.

Then there was silence; they had lost the scent.

Nobody saw which way the fox had gone. The other sabs appeared to our left; they stood still, not wanting to flush the fox out. The horn blew; the huntsman was calling his hounds out of the wood, back to the footpath – he couldn't hunt that fox with the police present and us filming. The hounds trotted off, noses to the ground, tails up. We stayed at the briar patch until the hunt had left the immediate area, and radioed, 'One away! Hunt headed south to Lockley Farm on footpath.'

'Well done, children!'

We extracted ourselves from the clawing brambles, ankles twisting on the rutted forest floor, throats throbbing, dry and hoarse, as we clambered out of the forest and followed the hoof prints south along the footpath. The two policemen re-joined us, 'You were not on a path when you were in there; you were trespassing.'

'We were on a path. Look at your maps.'

'We don't have any.'

'Then why do you think we were trespassing?'

'The terrier men told us.'

'And of course they wouldn't lie to you, would they? If you had followed us in, you would have seen we were

117

on a path. It was just a bit over-grown...'

At a crossroads in the track we examined the floor; quad bike marks went west, whilst paw prints and hoof marks went south. We split up. Three of us were running downhill after the horses and hounds, so fast with the aide of gravity that it felt like I was bound to fall as my heels thumped into the hard mud, jarring my knees, and I had to lean backwards so far to keep balanced that it made my spine ache. Then the path curved and went steeply uphill. My chest was tight and I couldn't seem to get enough air into my lungs. Running was now slow, my thighs burned and the bitter winter air stung my eyes.

The track levelled out. It forked again, three ways, and we each took a different path. We only had two radios between the whole group, with the base receiver being in the Landrover. As we three split now, only one of us had a radio. I continued to jog along the path. Up ahead I could see a red coat in the tree line. It was the hunt master with what looked like most of the hounds. I took out my phone, but there was no signal. The master of this hunt is dangerous; I know that from previous run-ins with him. I looked around, but could not see any sign of the police-men. A few of the hounds started crying. I shouted out, 'Sabs. Sabs. Sabs,' like an SOS call, hoping that someone would hear me and come to give me back up.

The hunt master came galloping along the track to-wards me. I retreated into the tree line. He shouted, 'Yeah you better get in those trees, or I will run you down. You're fucking vile.'

'I've got that on camera. Thanks!'

'You can have it on camera, I don't care, you troll.' He turned the horse into the trees towards me, and I backed away quickly. 'Where are you going? Go on, run, run.'

I tried to keep my camera up to record the threatening

118

behaviour, but it was hard as I needed both arms out to balance as I stumbled through the bracken. He kept pushing his horse through the brambles, and was barging me with the horse's chest.

'Oh you are a big man, aren't ya?' I mocked.

'I'm fucking sick of you lot!'

The horse was foaming at the mouth, his neck soaked in sweat. His legs were getting caught up in the spiked tendrils. The huntsman was jabbing on the reins, pulling the horse's head this way and that and kicking hard, trying to make it trample me.

'Hunt Master Liam Hakespear using his horse as a weapon.' It was another sab, standing a few feet away, filming and narrating for the benefit of the camcorder.

'Here's another one. Filthy lesbians. Get a job and fuck off!'

'You really are scum, aren't you?'

'Oh fuck off,' he shouted, livid with us for ruining his sport, and he spurred his horse on out of the brambles and took off.

We made our way after him as fast as we could, and happened across other foot sabs. They had seen the terrier men through the trees heading south-west and had radioed it in. We went in pursuit. We climbed over barbwire fences to find that the terrier men were parked up again and off their quads. They had their shovels out.

'What the fuck are you doing?' we asked, camcorders held up.

'This is private land. Fuck off.'

'What is this place called then, if it is private?'

'Pepper Harrow Park. You idiots don't even know where you are!'

Feigning sincerity, we asked, 'Show us on the map; if it is private we will leave.' We then radioed our position,

119

'Terrier men digging out a badger sett at Pepper Harrow Park, below where the 'w' of Harrow is on the map.'

'Copy that. Sending in the police.' We spoke for the benefit of the camera, 'You are clearly interfering with a badger sett. Badgers are protected, so private or not, you are breaking the law.' The head terrier man, Nick Colson, dropped his shovel and marched up to me. He is a good two feet taller than me, a skin head and very large; he must be more than twenty stone.

At the start of the season, I had been separated from the other sabs when the hunt tried to ride us down. I had ended up in a field on my own with Nick. He had mouthed off at me and was telling me about a fox they had killed the previous day.

'Didn't save that one, did ya?' he laughed.

I had retorted, 'You are nothing but a rich bit's lackey.'

Mistake.

This infuriated him and he turned scarlet with rage and squared up to me. His face was an inch from mine and he was screaming threats, his spittle covering me. I really thought I would end up face down in a ditch that day.

This time, he snatched the camera out of my hand and shoved me viciously to the ground. 'You are trespassing and I am using reasonable force to remove you.'

'You are a fucking bully, Nick! Decking a female half your size, that's something to be proud of.' He hissed, 'I will slit your throat and feed you to the hounds.'

I scrambled to my feet, but as I tried to stand upright he pushed me to the ground again.

'Get your hands off her, scum!' the other sabs were shouting out and jumped to my defence. There was a scuffle, and we were like rag dolls in the terrier men's grips. The rest of the sab group appeared with the police. Nick said, 'Get them out of here, they are trespassing.'

'He is interfering with a badger sett, and they are protected. Or do you think they are laying a trail through a badger sett? There is no reason for them to be here, at all, especially not with shovels. And he has stolen my property.'

'You are making it up. I don't want anything of yours.' The policemen reluctantly searched him. On finding my mini camcorder in his pocket, they questioned him.

'I found it on the floor. The stupid girl must have dropped it.'

The terrier men got back on their quads and sped off. We were cautioned that the next time we trespassed we would be arrested, and as it stood, we were cautioned and banned from re-entering the private Pepper Harrow Park for three months. Banned from somewhere we were never allowed to be in the first place? That's alright! We radioed the Commander, 'Quads gone south-west. We have lost the hunt. We are going to head for Britty Wood. We will make our way to the byway at Furze Hill for a pick up.'

'Copy that.'

Back in the truck we guzzled water and tended the bloody scratches on our hands and faces. We drove on down the byway looking for any sign of the hunt. A hunt support Range Rover was parked at an angle, blocking us from going forward. We edged nearer to it, trying to force it to move. The driver grinned at us, leaned out of his window and fired a catapult at us. The missile hit our windshield. 'Is someone filming?' yelled the Commander.

'Yes, we've got that on tape!'

121

'He is blocking us for a reason. All foot sabs out and get down there.'

We all piled out of the back and ran past the support vehicle. As we went, the driver was on his phone – calling the hunt master to tell them where we were. The Commander radioed through, 'All foot sabs on channel; the missile that was just fired at us was a metal ball bearing. Watch yourselves. Have called the cops, but they have left the area.'

We saw the hunt drawing a kale field in the valley below us. Maps indicated a bridle way that followed the perimeter of the field, so we split up, one group running left and one group right. We were so out-numbered that a fight would be quickly lost, although we were always prepared to take a beating if it meant saving the life of an innocent creature. And it is easier to press charges for assault than for illegal hunting, as long as you have some video footage that clearly shows the violence. Video footage that shows illegal hunting is explained away by the hunt; 'It was an accident. We tried to call the hounds off, but they didn't listen to us.'

We approached the main body of the hunt from both sides. They were standing around waiting for the hounds to pick something up in the field. We radioed in our position to the truck and one of the sabs called 999 from her mobile, pre-empting trouble, saying that we were going to go in to stop a kill and there would naturally be a breach of the peace, and that we were heavily out-numbered.

A quad bike then sped along the bridle path and into the field. It stopped, and one of the terrier men got off. He opened the wooden crate and pulled out an old feed sack. He called out to the hounds, 'Get up, get up, get up.' Having the attention of the hounds, he turned the sack upside down and a fox fell out. It crouched in the kale, stunned and confused. In a split second we looked at the hounds, saw them register the fox, and we charged forward to intercept them. We sprayed as we went, shouting 'Leave it! Leave it!' Back on his quad, the terrier man ran into me from behind, taking my right leg out from under me and knocking me to the floor.

This practice of bagging is common. The hunt master has to look good in front of the paying riders; he has to entertain them. If there is no chase, no kill, the riders will be disappointed and not ride with this hunt again. Early every morning hunt staff walk out in the fields behind the kennels. They put food out for the foxes. This encourages the foxes to stay in the area, and thereby provides the hunt with a good supply of live quarry to bag. They often catch pregnant vixens, because they cannot run very fast.

The screams were shrill and continuous. The writhing mass of hounds looked like a seething pile of maggots. The hounds were called off, and the hunt master rode over. He dismounted and cut the tail from the remains of the fox; his trophy for the day. He held it aloft to a chorus of great cheers.

We stood around the wide mess of blood, guts and red fur. Eight foetuses were identifiable by their clotting heads, scattered in the topsoil between the remnants of kale plants.

*   *   *

More than five hundred fox hunts go out in England every week. Despite it being an illegal activity, blood sports hunters continually flout the law and get away with it. The foxes need sabs to police the hunts, as the police aren't interested themselves. Please consider joining your local saboteur group. You can join as a driver, a navigator, a photographer, or a foot sab. You don't have to be a fast runner; your presence alone will help protect foxes from being murdered for sport. If you can't go out sabbing, consider fundraising for us. You can get the contact information of your local sab group from the Hunt Saboteurs Association, a nationwide organisation: www.hsa.enviroweb.org and info@huntsabs.org.uk.

Dan Widdowson 2012

The Liberation of Sadness

Michelle Williams

Ching Lan liked to explore. She spent hours wandering the dusty roads and countryside around her home, watching insects and smelling flowers.

She had always stayed well away from the shuttered warehouse that lay on the outskirts of the nearby city in an outfield, a formidable hulking building with wooden panels. Large trucks trundled noisily along the road every week, collecting whatever it was that the business pro-duced. Sometimes she heard strange noises coming from inside the warehouse; grunts and snorts that made her think of the largest dogs in the village, the ones that growled as she went by and scared her, even though they were tied up.

She was tired when she reached the borders of the ware-house plot one sweltering June day, and stopped to rest, out of sight behind a large boulder at the side of the road. She had seen a dirty green van parked just outside the gates, but thought nothing of it as she crouched down and stretched her weary, dusty legs out in front of her. From where she rested, she could hear the back of the van being opened, the clanging noise of chains hitting each other and a scraping sound as something large was dragged from the vehicle.

Resting her hands on the top of the rock, she slowly raised her head until half of her face was poking out above the boulder, enough for her to see what was happening. She watched as a large metal cage was pushed from the back of the van, roughly guided onto the ground by two burly men.

She ducked down as an unearthly sound cut through the air, a roar that struck her to the core. Trembling, Ching Lan battled to decide whether to stay or to run, curiosity eventually getting the better of her. She raised her head again and watched as the men lifted the cage. She could see what was inside.

The bear was small and black, a patch of creamy fur shaped like a crescent moon bright on its chest. It was cowering in the cage, its head low, licking a front paw that appeared to have been mangled. Blood was trickling down through the bars and dripping onto the yard.

The men took the cage through the open warehouse doors and disappeared inside.

Ching Lan sat for a while, unable to shake the image of the bear, thinking of the gentle eyes that had rolled in her direction, and seemed to have been pleading to her. That was silly, she knew… there was no way the bear could have seen her where she was hiding.

Before long, the men got back into the van and sped away, the wheels kicking up a plume of dust as they went past her, and she ducked around the other side of the rock to be sure she wasn't seen.

It was getting late and she would be expected home for dinner, but something was drawing Ching Lan towards the building that before had frightened her so much. Slowly, she walked towards the double doors, hesitating now and then, looking around in case anybody was watching her. Everything was quiet.

She tried to slide the doors open but they held fast, locked securely. Ching Lan told herself that was probably for the best. What if the noises she heard sometimes were the bears just roaming around in there, loose? If she opened the door she could end up being eaten.

She turned away, about to head home, when a grunting sound pulled her attention toward some movement seen from the corner of her eye, further along the side of the building. One of the wooden panels had come loose, the beam splintered and hanging. She crept over to the gap and squinted into the darkness. She could see metal bars, the chicken-wire mesh of a cage. She tentatively reached in and touched the bars, then jumped back as a large pink tongue snaked out from the darkness and lapped the tips of her fingers, rough and dry against her skin.

Through the gap, she watched as the bear shifted its weight, dappled black fur brushing along the bars, and an amber eye appeared, peering at her. The sad eye watched her, the iris contracting as it got adjusted to the light coming in.

She moved closer, but the bear flinched at the sound. She held out her fingers so that they didn't quite touch the bars. She knew wild animals were dangerous, knew not to get too close. But then again, the bear had just missed an opportunity to chomp down on her fingers and had instead chosen to lick them. She touched her thumb to the skin that had been touched by the tongue, remembered how dry it had felt.

A black nose poked through the bars and sniffed twice at her fingers, then the bear gave a harrumphing sigh and sank down to the bottom of the cage, out of sight.

'Are you thirsty?' Ching Lan whispered, the bear's nose was as dry as its tongue. She knew enough from time spent with dogs in her village to know that if their noses were grey and cracked, they needed water.

'I'll come back tomorrow. I'll bring you something,' she promised, then ducked away as dusk began to settle over the warehouse.

The next day Ching Lan woke up early. She snuck into the kitchen and found that her mother had been cutting hunks of watermelon into a bowl for breakfast. Delighted, Ching Lan snaffled up the bowl and hid it under her dress, the ceramic cold against her belly. She slipped from the house before anyone saw her.

The warehouse was quiet as she approached, and she ran to the broken panel, eager to see the bear. 'Psst!' she whispered, 'I've brought you something!'

She selected the largest piece of melon and held it up to the gap, waiting for the bear. She could tell he was there; she could hear the gruff exhalation of his laboured breathing. She listened as he rose slowly, sniffed twice and tentatively pushed his nose closer to the bars. She reached out, the watermelon bleeding precious juices that rolled down her wrist. 'Take it,' she urged, 'It's for you.'

Reluctantly, as if he was wary of a trick, the bear lapped gently at the fruit, then held back a moment as if he were afraid. Ching Lan reached out further, until the fruit was squashed up against the mesh.

The bear lowered his head, that beautiful amber eye appraising Ching Lan carefully. She could see her reflection in its glassy surface. The bear appeared to recognise her then, and pushed its mouth to her hand, its tongue lapping at the juice, tugging at the flesh with broken teeth. His gums were red-raw as if he had been smashed in the mouth.

'What shall I call you?' Ching Lan whispered, touching her fingertips to the bear's dry nose. Looking into his woeful amber eye, she could think of only one word for him: Sadness.

After a while, she left the bear and moved around the back of the buildings, searching for any other gaps in the wood. She was in luck. Right at the back she found a large wooden panel that had almost completely come loose. She pushed it with her hand and it slid up on its one remaining nail, leaving a gap just about large enough for her eight year old form to fit through.

The smell made her nose wrinkle up. She had smelled it a little outside, but inside the four walls it was intense; a mixture of animal faeces that hadn't been cleaned up for months and something else, something bitter and pungent.

There were cages everywhere. Most filled with bears that were too large for their man-made prisons. They hunkered down miserably, their spirits broken. Shocked, she saw that all the bears had little silver sticks poking out from their undersides. The tubes were imbedded into their flesh, the skin around the tubes weeping yellow pus. Ching Lan held her nose. She thought that the unusual smell must be coming from whatever was filling those tubes.

She stepped forward towards a cage and jumped back when the bear inside bashed a paw against the bar, warning her away. Frightened only for a moment, Ching Lan steeled herself and plucked a square of melon from the bowl. When the bear saw it he watched her approach, but did not make any move to take it. When Ching Lan was close enough to stroke the bear, not that she would have dared to, it slunk down to the bottom of the cage, despondent. Not wanting to distress it, she left the fruit just inside the bars and backed away a few steps. She stared at the bear's back, shocked at the sight of it. There was a criss-cross hatching print across the flesh, and most of the fur has been torn away, the bear's skin was angry and scabbed over. Ching Lan crouched, looking up to the top of the inside of the cage where a wire mesh had been suspended on ropes so that it could

131

be lowered when necessary. Chunks of flesh and fur were stuck in the metal hatchings. She realised miserably that the mesh must have been lowered onto the bear, possibly to hold him down. She shuddered and turned away.

Instantly she wished she hadn't.

On the other side of the room she saw the true purpose for the wire mesh. She approached the cage slowly, nausea burning her throat. The bear had its eyes closed and barely seemed to be alive. It was squashed down to the bottom of the cage by the mesh and the purpose of the casing appeared to be to squeeze the bear so tightly in the metal vice that the strange fluid poured freely from the tube that stuck out from the bear's belly. The liquid dripped into a dirty basin below.

The bear's skin had been cut by the wire of the mesh and the swollen flesh had moulded around it. Ching Lan realised that the bear had been left in this state for so long that the skin had begun to heal *over* the wire, the metal becoming a part of the bear. A violent red of rust and dried blood formed a shell on his back. The bear didn't seem to notice her presence at all, and when she nudged some melon towards its nose, it did not even flinch. It was almost comatose.

Horrified, she moved around the dingy cavern, holding out fruit to the bears one by one. Some were wary and unwilling to take it, whilst others lapped greedily at the pieces as if they hadn't eaten in months. Most of the bears looked starved; their ribs visible even through the course fur of their coats. Many had patches where their hair had been rubbed away against the bars. One of the bears was banging its head against the side of the cage, the only movement it had room to make. The sound of bone against metal resonated unnervingly; the bear's unfocused eyes and vicious self-abuse indicative of the fact that it had been tortured to the point of insanity.

Many of the bears had rotten teeth, broken like Sadness's but left to fester, the gums receding and lined with decay. Many couldn't even manage the fruit as their mouths were so sore.

Ching Lan realised that there wasn't one single bear in that room that hadn't been mistreated, that wasn't gravely wounded. Many had lost their front paws and the injuries had not been tended to, the stumps decomposing and yellow with pus. Some had bones protruding from the scarred flesh, and all of the bears were twisted unnaturally in their attempts to crouch without putting weight on their injured limbs.

Two of the bears looked towards her with unfocused eyes clouded with discolouration, blinking putrid pus, and she could tell with sorrow that they had become blinded by infection during captivity. Ching Lan held the melon to their noses so that they could smell it, determined not to allow them to go hungry because they couldn't see the food. When they tentatively opened their mouths and allowed her to feed them her heart leapt.

When Ching Lan's fruit bowl was empty and she had nothing to do but gaze, stupefied, she began to feel claustrophobic with the abject horror of the room. Her palms sweaty, her neck slick and itchy, her hair pasted to her skin.

She had to get out.

As she passed Sadness he gave a little snort of greeting. The stump missing a paw was fresh with new blood. She

133

kicked something as she passed and looked down in terror at the trap that had been slung carelessly beside the cage of its victim. The trap was made up of two rows of semicircular metal teeth, the teeth laced with blood and dust. Fur and torn flesh was stuck on the blades.

'I'll come back tomorrow, I promise,' Ching Lan wheezed, struggling to pull herself out through the hole and into the sunlight.

She tumbled through onto the ground outside and breathed in three large gulping breaths, her heart slamming against her ribcage. She was glad to be away from that foul air, away from the solemn eyes of the tortured bears.

Who would do such a thing, she wondered as she made her way back along the pathway, dizzy from her time in the acrid room. And what were those weird tubes sticking out of them? It looked like something from one of her brother's horror comics.

At home, she protested innocence over the theft of the watermelon, having hid the incriminating bowl under her bed. Later at supper she picked at her food.

'What's the matter, Ching Lan?' her father asked, putting down his chop sticks and staring intently at his youngest daughter. He knew her well and could tell when something was weighing on her mind.

She lifted her chin, frowning. 'Dad, what are bears used for?'

Surprised by the question, her father mirrored her frown. 'How do you mean?'

Ching Lan thought hard about her answer. She could not let her father know she had been snooping around where she didn't belong or he would be angry with her. And yet, she needed to know the truth. 'I know they are in the wild and sometimes they are pets and people make them dance for money.'

'Yes?'

Ching Lan momentarily recalled a dancing bear she had seen before at the market. A chain through its nose, the owner had whipped at the bears legs with bamboo to make it dance. She had thought nothing of it until now, realising that the sad look of the bears in the cages had been the same as the one worn by the bear who danced on the stony ground.

'Well, are there any other uses for them?'

Her father sighed, scratched his head distractedly. 'I can think of one other, Ching Lan. There is said to be something magical in the bears' body that is used to heal in medicines.'

'Magic?'

'The bears have something called a gall bladder. We have one too,' her father reached out and pushed his fingers against her middle. 'Farmers drain the fluid from the gall bladder of bears and it is used in medicines.'

'Does it work?'

'I don't know. I used to think so; ancient remedies are never really questioned, but I have been hearing a lot of different opinions recently. People are saying it doesn't work, that the people who sell the stuff are wrong because the bear bile can actually harm humans, and that in fact there are herbs that contain the same medicinal properties and work without any harmful effects on humans.'

So that's what the warehouse was, Ching Lan thought. A bear farm. And those funny tubes were taking away fluid from the bears' gall bladders. Fluid that did not even work.

Ching Lan's father was a perceptive man. He leaned forward and looked carefully at her. 'Ching Lan, do you know where our watermelon went this morning?'

135

She felt heat rush to her cheeks, giving her away.

'I know you wouldn't be able to eat all of that fruit by yourself. Where did you walk to today?'

Ching Lan felt tears prickle her eyelids. She pushed away her food. 'There is a bear farm in the warehouse along the road that leads to the big city,' she wept. 'I gave the fruit to the bears, because they are sad and hungry.'

She was crying hard now, but her father made no move to comfort her. 'Ching Lan, you know that to steal is bad. You also know that you aren't allowed to walk so far on your own. I'm disappointed in you. You are excused.'

Disgraced, Ching Lan fled to her room. She knew as she lay under the moonlight that bloomed in through the window that she should think about what she had done wrong, but all she could see when she closed her eyes was Sadness's gentle gaze, and the wounds and the misery on every bear in that warehouse. She slept fitfully, dreaming that she was locked in a cage, tubes penetrating her skin, a metal vice clamped tightly around her chest making it impossible to breath and searing wounds into her torso.

The next morning her mother stopped her from leaving the house, her tone cold. She asked for her bowl back and Ching Lan brought it to her, ashamed. Later in the afternoon she asked if she could take a walk, but was forbidden. 'You are staying here, young lady. You should be punished for your thievery.'

'But I promised!' she cried, thinking of Sadness waiting hopefully for her to come to him, his amber eye peeking through the gap in the wood... but finding no friends.

Her parents prevented her from leaving the house the next day, and the day after that. Ching Lan wept in her room

136

thinking of Sadness and the other bears, and the promise she had broken.

Eventually she was allowed to play outside, but was strictly forbidden to wander out of sight of the house. As desperate as she was to go back to the bears, she knew that she would be in terrible trouble if she broke the rules again.

A few weeks later her father shook her awake one morning, smiling down at her. 'I want you to come with me, Ching Lan,' he said, his eyes bright with excitement.

She rubbed her sleep-crumbed eyes. 'Where are we going?'

'You'll see.'

She dressed quickly and followed her father out into the cool morning air, holding his hand as he led her along the roadway towards the city. When they passed the market-place she saw the man with the dancing bear and had to turn away, tears in her eyes. She knew the bear should be free and roaming the land, not stuck with a ring in its nose being mercilessly whipped for people's fleeting enter-tainment.

'It's not right, is it?' her father asked, following her gaze.

She shook her head, thankful that her father could see the injustice, too.

It wasn't long before she realised where they were going. She looked up at her father, open-mouthed. 'This is the way to the bear farm.'

'Yes, it is.'

Excitement bubbled up inside her. She quickened her pace, tugging at her father's arm in an attempt to make him hurry. He laughed and sped up a little, humouring her.

'When you told me about the farm that day, I thought long and hard about it. I undertook research, and read as much as I could about bear farms. It seems the bears are caught, often from the wild, in vicious traps that cause them to lose their paws.'

'Yes, I've seen that, Father,' Ching Lan told him, picturing Sadness and the other bears who had lost their paws.

Her father met her eyes, he seemed unsettled that she had witnessed such a thing. 'The bears are then subjected to torturous techniques to extract the bile.' He shook his head, sadly. 'It seems a pointless and brutal activity when the bile itself is useless, used by ancient witchdoctors but proven to have no merit. Remember when Grandma told us about the old medicine man in her village selling the souls of the men who had been hanged?'

Ching Lan knew how silly that notion was.

'It made me think of that, Ching Lan. The idea of selling a hanged man's soul is just ridiculous. I learned from my friend Dr Ping at the university that the bear bile is likely to contain cancer cells, urine and faeces. Not to mention infection. Imagine drinking something like that? Do you think it would cure you, or make you ill?'

Ching Lan wrinkled her nose; expecting this liquid to cure anything was just as ridiculous and her grandma's tale.

Her father sighed and shook his head. 'Dr Ping suggested I contact an organisation that rescues the bears from illegal farms.'

Ching Lan stopped in her tracks, kicking up dust. 'But the person who owns them wouldn't let them do that, would he?'

Smiling, her father nodded. 'It is illegal to bear farm in this province, I am pleased to say. He had no choice.'

Ching Lan cheered and spun round in a circle, barely able to believe her ears.

'We are one of the few provinces that bear farming is illegal in. There are still many places where the bear farms thrive, more bears being subjected to torture every day.' As he spoke Ching Lan's face fell, her elation short lived.

They walked on and Ching Lan could see the warehouse, a number of vehicles parked up outside, and people swarming around the building. As they got closer she could make out a logo that appeared on the side of the vans; *Animals Asia.*

She tugged her hand from her father's grip and ran to one of the vehicles, skidding to a halt as a cage was brought out of the warehouse. A familiar bear lay prostrate on a tarpaulin inside it. 'Sadness!' Ching Lan cried, 'He's dead!'

A woman stepped forward and placed a hand on the girl's shoulder. 'No, he's alright. We've just sedated him for the journey.'

Ching Lan wiped tears from her face with the back of her wrist. 'Where are you taking him?'

'To a wonderful place. A sanctuary where he will be fed and kept in comfort for the rest of his life.'

Sniffing, reassured, Ching Lan reached out and stroked the one intact fore-paw that flopped from the cage. 'Goodbye, Sadness.'

'Sadness?' the woman asked, turning to her as the bear was carefully loaded into the back of the truck. 'Is that what you call him?'

Ching Lan nodded. 'It was the only name I could think of. He just looked so sad.'

The woman looked back at the bear and then turned to Ching Lan with a warm smile. She crouched down beside her. 'You know, we like our bears to have positive names, because that's where we are taking them, to a life that is more positive. In a few weeks time, when this bear has been treated by our vets and made to feel much better, when he's clean and fed well and allowed to roam around in a lovely grassy area with other bears around him, what do you think he will look like then?'

Ching Lan thought of Sadness roaming around, playing with other bears, fruit and water in abundance. She smiled. 'I think he will be happy.'

'Well, then. If you don't mind, I think I'd like to call this bear Happiness.'

Ching Lan nodded, smiling.

She stood with her father and watched as the other bears were taken from the darkness of the warehouse and loaded carefully into the vehicles that would take them to safety, to medical attention and a new life.

As the last van pulled away, she lifted her hand and waved. 'Bye, Happiness,' she whispered, and smiled.

Lucy Thornton 2012

They Came Home to Die

Elizabeth C. Koubena

Those of us who work in animal welfare in Greece have seen many animals die of poisoning.

I have lost count of those I have held in my arms, hoping treatment would save them and trying to comfort them, and feeling helpless in the face of their pain. It is a heartbreaking experience one never gets used to. Here is one story...

When we moved to the island of Aegina in 1996, we adopted the stray dogs of our neighbourhood. Scarlet had been a local stray for years, and she and her mate, Mouchli, had had a litter of puppies just before we took up residence. We began feeding Scarlet, realising that she was also feeding puppies. Mouchli was always by her side, but we could never find the puppies... until one day they simply walked up our dirt road. There were four of them; big, fat, healthy darlings. One brown, one black, one white and one mixed; we called them Choco, Blackie, Bimbo and Fred.

The neighbours were all quite fond of the dogs; they had known Scarlet for years and she had given birth many times. What happened to those puppies you might well ask. Our neighbours were holidaying summer residents and had no idea. I did. How Scarlet escaped the annual culling of strays by poison is a mystery. She had a seventh sense about poisoned food I think, and she never touched it. Mouchli was also a survivor. He and I became great friends.

We cooked all summer for that brood of dogs. In September the summer residents went back to the city and we

143

remained the only people in the area. The pups grew older and more adventurous and even though we had a walled-in yard, it wasn't difficult for the dogs to get out, following their parents on their habitual wanderings.

By February, the puppies were nine months old and B-I-G dogs. We had made a sleeping area for them in the yard. We had had Scarlet neutered by then, so there was no danger of more puppies; she seemed relieved and determined to enjoy time together with her last litter.

It was a cold winter's day. I hadn't seen the dogs all day and it was almost dinner-time so I wondered where they were. My husband decided to look around the neighbourhood. When he returned, he was carrying Bimbo in his arms. 'He's been poisoned,' he said. We rushed into action – salt and water to induce vomiting and after he threw up pieces of sausage, we gave him atropine injections. Then we covered him up and went out to find the others. A little further down the same road we came upon Mouchli. The two of us carried him home and repeated the treatment.

My husband went out to find the others while I phoned the vet for more instructions, and made the two dogs as comfortable as I could. Then Scarlet returned home, with no signs of being poisoned. She watched in silence as I continued treatment on the two boys.

My husband returned empty-handed. We looked for them in the coming days, but we never found the other three dogs.

Bimbo was the first to die. We cried as we wrapped him up in a clean white sheet and laid him on the terrace. We continued to treat Mouchli, but he was weakening. We had hooked him up to an intravenous drip and I was adjusting it when he made a noise; a low rumbling sort of sound. I knew he was telling me to let him go. I removed the needle and sat beside him cradling his head in my arms. He opened his eyes and with one last look at me, he signed, closed his eyes, went into a coma and died.

We buried them with honour. That was eight years ago. As I write this story, I am crying at the merciless murder of five sweet dogs. Scarlet mourned too; she sat on the terrace day after day, barely eating, never leaving the house. I would sit beside her and sing her songs, silly perhaps, but I wanted to cheer her up. She stayed this way until May and then one night we had a party and everyone made a great fuss over her and she decided life was worth living. She continued to live with us for five and a half more years until her death from cancer in November 2002. But she lives on, on the cover of a number of S.P.A.Z. brochures and we remember her and her family with great fondness.

I ask myself how has it happened that in a country that gave birth to democracy; a humane philosophy of life, to magnificent literature still read and still relevant today, how does a country that has honoured the great human spirit, and in this the 21st century, routinely practice the cowardly and cruel act of poisoning unwanted animals? It is, of course, against the law to murder animals, but identifying people who poison is difficult; they do it in secret and go to great lengths not to be caught doing it. It is also believed that authorities carry out mass slaughter to clear their area of strays.

This is a sad story but it is part of the reality of living in Greece. I fight against poisoning animals by carrying my

145

anti-poison kit around with me, as well as the cell phone number of my vet, by protecting my own animals as best I can and by lobbying and campaigning to stop this barbaric practice.

And one day it will stop.

Mouchli and the Boys by Elizabeth C. Koubena

Mortimer Sparrow 2012

The Circle of Life

Susan Loose

As I walked the green lanes near my home, I regularly passed a sprig of elm which stuck out across the path. Feeding on this branch was a bunch of happy black and white caterpillars. They looked a bit like bird droppings at a glance, but on closer inspection I could see them move as they chomped away at the leaves.

At first I'd thought the branch was hazel, and it was only on looking up the caterpillars in a field guide, finding that they were comma butterfly larva, and that one of their food plants was elm, that I looked more closely at the plant itself. The leaves of the elm tree, although very similar in shape to hazel, have a slightly less coarse, hairy feel to them; and there is a difference in the way the leaf is attached to the stem, although to be honest I still find it hard to distinguish between the two, unless I have them side by side. Obviously it's not so for the comma; they know where to lay their eggs.

Each day the holes in the leaves got larger and the caterpillars got fatter and fatter, and one by one they disappeared, until only one was left. This one lone, fat caterpillar decided to pupate right on the end of the branch – the part that was sticking out across the path. I watched, entranced, as the soft, nondescript larva transformed into an alien-looking, dark-brown spiky case; rather like a dead leaf, but with two tiny, bright-silver mirror-like spots. It hung firm, dangling quietly and securely from a leaf at head height.

Although obviously human life went on, I developed a real attachment to the budding butterfly. I walked the path again, looking forward to seeing my transformed friend, safe on the underside of its leaf. Horrifyingly, I found carnage instead; very recently a tractor had been along and the hedge-cutter had flailed the foliage, which now lay battered and shredded on the path. To my relief, only the hedge on one side of the lane had been cut so far, and it wasn't the side where my pupa still hung… safe… for now.

My principles are generally not to interfere with Nature, but the hedge-cutter would obviously come back soon to complete the job. Besides, the mechanical decimation of hedges is not a natural phenomenon. With no hesitation, I plucked the leaf stem and its hanging jewel and returned home quickly.

What was I to do now?

It was like suddenly being left with a baby, with no idea of its needs and no way to communicate. Thanks to the Internet, in a short time I knew all I could about rearing a butterfly, and more about commas and their habits than I had thought possible.

I contacted a friend with young children and an interest in wildlife, whose son, he said, would love to hatch my treasure, and who conveniently had an unheated, dry shed; the ideal place, according to my research. Jonathan is a singer and songwriter, and I tentatively handed over the pupa at the end of a music festival we both attended that weekend. I knew the pupa would receive the best of care and attention, but still had doubts in human ability to replicate natural conditions sufficiently for it to survive and act out its final metamorphosis.

About three weeks later I was reeling from losing Prince, my twenty-eight-year-old horse, who had been my companion for twenty-five years. I'd bought him shortly after moving to North Wales at the age of eighteen, and together we had explored all the bridle-paths and tracks of the Ceiriog Valley. He helped me come to know and love the area where I lived.

This day the weather was dire and I was passing time indoors, keeping busy with work on the computer. I opened an email to find the pupa had hatched! My friend had returned from the school-run with his kids and had opened the shed to find a perfectly formed butterfly, resting next to its empty larval-case, drying its wings. As soon as Amelia (as the children had named her, and they were sure she was female) was fully dry, she started to flutter to the window, trying to get to the light. Miika, on the advice of his dad, gently caught her, took her through the door, and released her to fly skyward. She headed for the near-by hills, and a safe place to hide for the winter, probably with the underside of her wings camouflaged against the bark of a tree, as I had read most commas do.

That night I dreamt of flying horses with butterfly wings. Prince was safe amongst their number, his brilliant chestnut coat and flaxen mane merged beautifully with the autumnal-gold colours of the comma wings with which he flew.

I woke in the morning feeling strangely peaceful. It came to me that this is what it's all about; the circle of Life and Death – as one thing passes, another comes into being.

In nature, nothing is ever wasted and everything is inter-connected.

In a way, sad as I am, I'm relieved by Prince's passing. I had struggled with his aging and infirmity and had questioned my ability to provide care for him as time went on and he became more and more infirm. Had I thought, all those years ago, of the time and money involved in owning a horse for its lifetime, would I have taken it on?

Now my responsibilities will be to the natural world around me, and my joy will come from helping wild creatures to be free... with maybe a little extra help now and then if needed.

Chris Ledward 2012

Two Guardian Angels

Jane Biehl

It feels like toothache when I think about the loss of my mother.

I cautiously touch the spot to see if the pain is still there... I always feared her death, and of being left alone... but Mom unexpectedly left behind a guardian angel: Sita, my hearing dog.

My mother and I were extremely close. She proudly told everyone we met that I was not only her daughter, but also her best friend. My father is dead, my siblings live out of state and I am single, never married and with no children. My mother and I relied on each other for support. She lived next door to me for six years after my father was placed in a nursing home. She later moved to an assisted living scheme and finally into a nursing home herself.

I have severe hearing loss and have lived alone for thirty-eight years. Without my hearing aids, I am unable to hear the doorbell, telephone or fire alarms. For years Mom had urged me to get a hearing dog, but I had constantly postponed it with the usual excuses of being too busy or protesting that others needed a dog more than I did. The catalyst for getting a dog was when a deaf friend was robbed and severely beaten... he couldn't hear the criminal entering the house.

A friend suggested Circle Tail. I clicked on the website and experienced a gut reaction – *this place is meant for me!* I read about their unique program, where dogs are rescued and then trained in prisons to become service dogs. One story jumped off the page at me; a testimony written by a prisoner about a particular dog he had trained. He explained that the bright-eyed beauty had opened his 'hard heart' and he hoped whoever received this wonderful creature would love the dog as much as he did. So I contacted Circle Tail, completed a lot of paperwork and passed a home visit. I was informed that the usual waiting period for a dog is between twelve and eighteen months.

The training of these special assistance dogs is intense. Circle Tail's executive, Marlys Staley, started with a dream that turned into a wonderful reality; most of the dogs acquired are rescues. Many of them are saved from being put down in local pounds. A few are donated by breeders, unwanted. The dogs are trained in four different prisons. Why in prisons? Most other people are too busy working, going to school, and performing daily tasks to be involved with a dog 24/7. The canines eat with the prisoners, go to the exercise yard with them and sleep in bed crates in the cells with them at night.

Gradually dogs are weeded out of the program; they are eliminated for reasons such as chasing a cat while in vest, or being too timid in challenging situations. These dogs are eventually adopted; Circle Tail arranges adoptions for over two-hundred-and-fifty dogs a year to good homes. The few unique dogs that are not easily intimidated, are very obedient, and have laid back personalities are taken to foster homes, where they are trained for specific in-house tasks; a dog training to help a person in a wheelchair is taught to open doors and cabinets, whilst hearing dogs are trained to bump the owner if a phone rings or someone is at the door.

Meanwhile, future owners are being carefully selected for the dogs. My guardian angel was busy in training long before I realised I needed a dog. I was busy counselling students and children. It was obvious I would need a laid back dog that loved people. Since this was my first experience with a dog, I also needed one that was forgiving and very easy to work with.

Visiting Circle Tail, I watched in amazement as fifteen people worked with dogs on leashes. They were going around in a huge circle much like the obedience classes I have seen in other places, but this circle was different. The dogs had to go through tunnels, walk on a thin rail, step on a swaying bridge and slide under bars. Marlys was in the centre giving instructions to the owners, who then instructed the dogs and helped them understand what was being asked of them.

A foster mother placed a leash in my hand. I looked down at a slightly built yellow lab-mix. She stood tall and proud and gazed up at me; an exquisite expression crossed her face as her brows furrowed. She bore an expression of sweetness and softness that drew me to her. Her face was finely sculptured and dainty looking. Her nose wasn't the typical black seen on most dogs, but a pinkish colour. Her fur was a light yellow, reminding me of rays of gentle sunshine. She had one little mole on the side of her face which added to her attractiveness – it gave her a beauty-star look – but the dog's most compelling feature was her deep eyes. When she gazed at me I was mesmerized – I could see her soul. Her eyes were not quite brown nor green, but brilliant amber and they swallowed me up. Our bonding started there and then.

I was smitten.

Sita and I went around the obstacle course for over an hour. She obeyed every command and was eager to please me. She had a quiet and calm personality. I walked over to Marlys and said, 'Sita is getting tired. And I am getting very attached to her. Who does she belong to?'

Marlys smiled, 'You, now.'

Once the decision was made to match Sita and me, we needed to learn to work as a partnership. I returned a month later for intense training with her. She stayed overnight with me at the hotel, and a trainer showed me what to do with her when I went to restaurants, grocery stores and public places. I was given a list of more than fifty commands she had learned. The Americans with Disabilities Act was explained to me in case I was ever challenged about taking her somewhere that dogs are not allowed. I read books and watched instructional movies and learned more than I had in my doctoral program at college!

I finally brought Sita home and took her to meet my mother. By this time, Mom was unable to take care of herself. She was in an assisted living apartment. My astonishment at Sita's sensitivity grew; my mother was sitting in her chair with a large walker in front of her. Sita carefully went around the walker and kissed my mother on the face. The next day she crawled under the walker and greeted her with her nose. Sita knew instinctively that one false move could cause Mom to fall and was always careful.

Sita and I went to visit my mother every day, and we took Mom out to eat at least five times a week. Sita was always gentle and greeted Mom with a wagging tail and joyful kisses. The special relationship between Mom and my assistance dog was obvious to anyone who watched them.

The other residents and staff in the assisted living facility looked forward to Sita's visits.

Sita opened up so many doors for me. She forced me to go outdoors and enjoy nature with her. We went on play dates with other dogs and made wonderful new friends who were doggy lovers. In my private practice as a counsellor, she comforted the hurting children who had been abused and abandoned.

One day I was attempting to console a client who was sobbing in my office. Neither one of us were paying any attention to Sita, who was lying down under my desk. To my utter astonishment, Sita got up, trotted over to my desk and pulled a tissue out of the box with her mouth and gave it to my client. My client said, 'Sita, you made my day!' and we both ended up laughing. She was a therapy dog as well as a hearing dog and she accompanied me every-where. She taught me with her wonderful kisses and playful attitude to seize the moment.

I regaled Marlys and the people from Circle Tail with stories about this amazing dog. I was delighted when they told me that my Sita was the dog the prisoner had talked about on the website. Sita, with her gentle nature, has influenced so many people on her journey.

My mother became progressively weaker in the following year. One evening she told me over and over again, 'Sita is the best thing that ever happened to you. She will take care of you after I am gone. You are probably tired of hearing me say that.'

I replied, 'No, I'm not tired of hearing it, because it is true.'

Two days later, I received a call from the nursing home: Mom had suffered a stroke and was paralyzed. When Sita and I entered her room she was conscious and in terrific pain. I called relatives; a cousin came to be with me. My mother showed her love to the end, being more worried that I was witnessing her pain than the fact that she was suffering so much. I held Mom and told her I loved her as she drew her last breath. I pushed back my tears until she was gone, and then sobbed hysterically. Sita sat faithfully by my side and never moved.

When I entered the nursing home a few days later to pick up my mother's belongings, a nurse took me aside. She told me, 'You did not see your dog because you were taking care of your mother. I was watching the dog and when she died, that dog knew. The saddest look came across that dog's face. I went home that night and told my husband – *that dog knew.*'

I miss my mother dearly, and there is not a day I don't think about her with love. But I realised the cycle of life continued for me. After my father died, my mother and I had had each other. After my mother's death, I had Sita. I am never really alone.

A year after my mother's death, I was diagnosed with a serious and potentially fatal illness. Sita was there when the doctor told me the average life expectancy was a few years. I was devastated and anxious. The next few months were very difficult, as I adjusted to doctor's visits, chemo and tests.

Sita's personality began to change. Her tail wagged less often. She refused to give kisses to me. She became over-protective. One day I was with a friend, who is a master dog trainer. Two dogs approached me and Sita snapped at them. I became distraught, afraid of not being able to keep Sita; no-one is allowed to keep a dog that is aggressive. My friend explained, 'Sita is picking up on all of your emotions. You are upset and she senses it. If you calm down, she will.' It hit me like a ton of bricks. All I can do is take care of myself and control my emotions. I started to be calmer, and began to take every single moment as it came. We only have today; yesterday is gone and tomorrow has not arrived. Sita and I developed an ever stronger bond and we enjoy every minute together.

As I watch Sita at work and at play, I am enjoying life myself. She has flown with me all over the country. She plays every night with a neighbour dog, a black lab named Max. To watch these two dogs play and enjoy every second with abandon brings me happiness that nothing else can. Sometimes I treat her to a sweet dish and she tastes every bite as if it is her last one. She is smart enough to know all we ever have is the present and to cherish it, and truly that is the most important lesson of life.

Thank you my guardian angel and thank you Mom!

Dan Widdowson 2012

The Boy and the Starfish

Adapted from an anonymous fable by Jenny Elliott-Bennett

Whilst walking along a beach in the heavy midday sun, an elderly man saw something in the distance. Getting nearer, he could see that someone up ahead was leaning down, picking things up and then throwing them into the ocean. As he got closer, he saw the figure was that of a young boy. The boy was picking starfish up, one by one, and tossing each one gently back into the water.

The old man approached the boy and said, 'Hello. May I ask what it is that you are doing?'

The boy looked up and replied, 'I'm throwing starfish into the sea.'

The old man smiled and said, 'Yes, but why are you throwing starfish into the sea?'

The boy said, 'The sun is hot and the tide is out. If I don't throw them back into the water, they'll die.'

The old man's eyebrows raised and he laughed. Gesturing up and down the beach, he said 'Young man, there are miles and miles of beach and there are starfish along every mile. You can't possibly make any difference at all!'

The boy was silent. He looked hard into the old man's eyes. Then he bent down, picked up another starfish from the scorched sand, walked a few feet into the surf and carefully dropped the starfish back into the water. He turned to the old man and said, 'I made *all* the difference to that one.'

The Authors

Teresa Ashby lives in Essex. Her short stories and serials have been published in magazines in the UK and abroad and some of her short story collections and novellas are available to buy on Kindle. She is a vegetarian who greatly admires the dedication of those who work so hard for the welfare of animals. Find her on Twitter @TeresaAshby and on Blogger at http://teresaashby.blogspot.co.uk

Jane Biehl PhD, PCC, MA has experience in several professions and has been a librarian, a clinical counsellor, a teacher and a writer. Currently she is a faculty member at a community college teaching Deaf Culture and Interpreting in an American Sign Language Certification program. She has had many articles published in various publications including *Ohio Media Spectrum; Self Help for Hard of Hearing Magazine; American Rehabilitation Counselling Bulletin; Deaf American Monograph; Hearing Loss Magazine; Partners Forum* and several books published by Happy Tails Publishing Company. She also authored a book published by S and J Publishing Company titled *Here to Bump and Bump to Hear* on her hearing ear dog, Sita. Biehl resides in North Canton, Ohio USA with her rescue cat, Cesar and dog, Sita. She enjoys writing, reading, and travel and conducts many programs educating people about assistance and service dogs. Her website is www.sitaandjane.com and she can be reached by email: Jane.M.Biehl@gmail.com

Pat Black is a journalist and author who lives in East Yorkshire, England, although he was born and brought up in Scotland. When he's not driving his missus to distraction with all the typing, he enjoys hill walking, fresh air and the natural world, and can often be found sweating on the hills and being polite to livestock in the Lake District. His short stories have been published in several anthologies and have won prizes including the Daily Telegraph's Ghost Stories competition. He has also been shortlisted for the Red Cross International Prize and the Bridport Prize. He is currently working on his latest novel, *Post*.

Sarah Brown is co-founder of the brilliant vegan-run animal rescue in mid Wales, Forget-Me-Not Animal Rescue. They have over fifty rescued animals and many wildlife species living on the land. Forget-Me-Not Animal Rescue is one of the organisations that will benefit from the sale of this book. For more information, see the Introduction.

Hemal de Silva is a Sri Lankan agriculturist trying his best to promote the growing of Pentadesma Butyracea, which has the potential to create a cleaner environment and alleviate poverty, for the benefit of the people and wildlife in rural areas. He enjoys seeing wild animals in their natural habitat.

Contact: hsdes59@yahoo.com

Jennifer Domingo works in a library and lives with her cat, Charlie, in Hertfordshire. In her spare time she likes people watching, day dreaming and keeping up with her blog. She's very happy to have five other short stories and one haiku published in various anthologies so far!

Jenny Elliott-Bennett BA Hons, MA, PGCE PCET is a qualified teacher and freelance writer, producing aca-demic, corporate and commercial copy that has been published in six countries in print and online. She is a vegan animal rights campaigner, a hunt saboteur and an animal freedom activist. She lives by the sea with an old blind cat rescued from death row.

Contact: comeinbennett@hotmail.com

Catherine Ione Gray started writing in her early teens and has never stopped. She lives in Nottinghamshire, although she was born and raised in Michigan, USA. She enjoys spending time pottering in the garden, reading novels and writing her own, not always in that order. Three of her novels are due to be published by the end of 2012.

Elisabeth Key is PR and Communications Manager at International Animal Rescue and has worked for the charity for the past eight years. Prior to that she spent ten years at the International Fund for Animal Welfare, and wrote numerous letters and articles for the national press in support of the campaign to ban hunting with dogs. Elisabeth lives in Kent with her husband, teenage son and two rescued Great Danes, Leo and Jasper. She can be contacted on lis@internationalanimalrescue.org

Elizabeth Koubena lives in Greece. While it's a beautiful country, the grim reality of millions of stray animals is impossible to ignore. She became involved twenty-five years ago with the Society for the Protection of Stray Animals (Athens) and has been doing rescue work, neutering, fund-raising, lobbying and writing about animals (and painting them) ever since. She and her husband live with eighteen cats and four dogs (all rescues) and feed a group of twelve village cats (all neutered). The work is hard sometimes but they also feel privileged to share their lives with so many wonderful animals.

Contact: elizkou@hotmail.com

Sue Loose lives in North Wales where she runs her own animal-sitting and gardening business and spends any spare time working to protect the countryside and wildlife she loves, including six acres which she manages specifically to encourage biodiversity.

John Roberts was a financial journalist and broadcaster. Today he knowingly writes fiction. Expelled from school, he started as a newspaper van boy and during the career that followed wrote two books, *Megalomania, Managers & Mergers* (Pitman Longman, 1987) and, explaining the foreign exchange markets to the layperson, *$1,000 Billion a Day* (Harper Collins, 1995 and Japanese rights sold). Now he collects agents' rejections of his novel… but when they come by email, can't even use them as wallpaper.

Madeleine Sara has, over the years, indulged her passion for writing through self-published websites, magazines and a 'How to' book *Fiddly Little Fingers and Tricky Toes*. She's had sixteen non-fiction articles published in national magazines. In 2009, she started writing poems, took a creative writing course and began blogging: http://scribbleandedit.blogspot.com. Since then she's had haiku, flash fiction and short stories accepted for publication. She also launched an eBook short story, *Ultimate Sacrifice* in 2012.

Mortimer Sparrow can be contacted via:
www.facebook.com/MortimerSparrowArt

Patricia Stoner has been a journalist, advertising copywriter and publicist. Now retired, she is strictly a hobby writer, although her creative writing group keeps her on her toes. She is the author of *Paws and Whiskers*, a collection of humorous verse about cats, which is available from Amazon in Kindle format. Her published work also includes short stories and poems in various anthologies and flash fiction featured on the Writers Billboard website.

Contact: sussexwriters@hotmail.co.uk

Steve Wade is an Irish writer and English language teacher. A prize nominee for the PEN/O'Henry Award, 2011, and a prize nominee for the Pushcart Prize, 2013, his fiction has been published widely in print and online. His work has won awards and been placed in prestigious writing competitions, including being shortlisted among five in the Wasafiri Short Story Prize 2011, a nomination for the Hennessy New Irish Writer Prize, and Second Place in the International Biscuit Publishing contest, 2009. His novel *On Hikers' Hill* was awarded First Prize in the UK abook2read Literary Competition, December 2010 – among the final judging panel was the British lyricist Sir Tim Rice. His fiction has been published in over twenty-five print publications, including New Fables, Gem Street, Grey Sparrow, Fjords Arts and Literary Review, and Aesthetica Creative Works Annual.

Contact: www.stephenwade.ie

Michelle Williams is twenty-nine years old and lives in the historic city of Lancaster with her partner, Russ and their many pets. She loves to write and has had a great deal of success this year, coming second in the Momaya Review and runner up in the Stringybark Australian History anthology, Chapter One Promotions romantic fiction prize and The Word Hut competition. She has supported the moon bears and Animals Asia for a number of years and is thrilled to be able to raise awareness of their excellent work. When she isn't writing, Michelle loves to play pool, read and paint. She can be contacted for commission work: <u>chelle8854@yahoo.co.uk</u>

The Artists

Edd Cross is a freelance cartoonist and illustrator, enjoying life in Brisbane, Australia, where he takes inspiration from local flora and fauna. Edd is a self-taught artist and just loves to draw; he always has a pencil and sketchbook at hand wherever he goes. Edd has created colouring-in sheets for environmental organisations, self-published his own mini comics and zines, and provides cartoon workshops. For more information please see http://eddcross.blogspot.com or email Edd directly: eddcross_artist@ymail.com.

Christopher Ledward is a British artist and freelance illustrator, living and working in Devon. Following a Foundation course at Exeter, he went on to study Illustration at the Arts Institute in Bournemouth, during which time he founded the Institute's monthly comic magazine, *Kpow!* Working across a variety of medium and with wide-ranging subjects, Ledward takes inspiration from current events, daily observations and other people's travel diaries. Most recently, his illustrations have been featured in Little White Lies magazine and ChefsMove.org, and his work is regularly showcased, both locally and nationally. He is currently working on a personal project centred on the 1920s, to culminate in a self-published limited edition book and print series.

Contact: chris.ledward@gmail.com or see the website www.chrisledward.co.uk

Mortimer Sparrow can be contacted via: www.facebook.com/MortimerSparrowArt

Kate Tacey is thirteen years old and studying at Leehurst

Swan School on an Art Scholarship. She has won awards for her work. Kate lives with her family in Wiltshire.

Lucy Thornton BA (Hons) Visual Communication Design offers animal portraits and general illustration. Located in North Yorkshire, she loves art, animal rights and wildlife. Contact: lucythornton71@gmail.com

Dan Widdowson studies illustration at the Arts University College, Bournemouth. The moment he heard about the opportunity to illustrate for a project that would help animals he knew that he had to get involved. As a vegan and an advocate of animal rights, he thinks there is no better use for his drawings than projects like this. It is his hope that he can combine his love of illustration with his passion for animal rights to create and inspire change. He can be contacted on: dan.widdowson@live.co.uk and his current portfolio can be found at: http://danwiddowson.crevado.com

Other Publications by Bridge House

Gentle Footprints

Gentle Footprints is a wonderful collection of short stories about wild animals. The stories are fictional but each story gives a real sense of the wildness of the animal, true to the Born Free edict that animals should be born free and should live free. The animals range from the octopus to the elephant, each story beautifully written.

Gentle Footprints includes a new and highly original story by Richard Adams, author of *Watership Down*, and a foreword by the patron of Born Free, Virginia McKenna OBE.

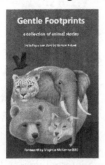

£1 from the sale of each copy, plus a percentage of the author royalties, will be donated to The Born Free Foundation.

This special book will raise both awareness and much-needed funds for the animals. Check out the Gentle Footprints blog which includes links and information from Born Free about each of the featured animals. Find out how you can get involved in their conservation:
http://gentlefootprintsanimalanthology.blogspot.com

Order from www.bridgehousepublishing.co.uk

ISBN 978-1-907335-04-4

Wild n Free

A collection of wild animal stories by children aged 9-16 years

These are the short-listed stories from the PAWS Children's Animal Writing Competition 2011, judged by Virginia McKenna OBE and children's writers Lauren St.John and Alan Gibbons. The stories really capture the essence of the wild animal. All royalties will be donated to the animal charity, The **Born Free Foundation**.

Born Free is a dynamic international wildlife charity, devoted to compassionate conservation and animal welfare. Born Free believes wildlife belongs in the wild and works to phase out zoos and stop animal exploitation. Born Free rescues individuals and gives them lifetime care. With local communities, Born Free protects lions, elephants, tigers, gorillas, wolves, bears, dolphins, turtles and many more species in their natural habitat. Find out more at www.bornfree.org.uk|

Order from www.pawsnclawspublishing.co.uk